Enid B

D0120994

Those Dreadful Children

AWARD PUBLICATIONS LIMITED

For further information on Enid Blyton please visit *www.blyton.com*

ISBN 978-1-84135-646-4

Illustrated by Ray Mutimer
Cover illustration by Leo Hartas

First published 1949 by Lutterworth Press
First published by Award Publications Limited 1999
This edition first published 2010

Published by Award Publications Limited,
The Old Riding School, The Welbeck Estate,
Worksop, Nottinghamshire, S80 3LR

10 1

Printed in the United Kingdom

Contents

1

At the Bottom of the Garden

Two children stood on a garden roller at the bottom of their garden. A third one tried to get up too, but there was no room for her.

'Let me up,' she wailed. 'I want to see too.'

'Wait,' said the others. 'We'll let you see in a minute.'

The two on the garden roller were looking up the garden of the house that was built at the bottom of their garden. The two gardens joined at the foot. The children's garden was neat and trim and full of flowers. The other garden was untidy and overgrown.

'They've gone, Marian,' said John, her brother. 'The curtains are down. The garden seat is gone. The house is empty.'

'Let me *see*!' cried Annette, scrabbling at their legs. 'You're horrid! Let me see too!'

Mrs Carlton came down the garden, hearing Annette's voice. 'Oh, let her see,' she said. 'She's so much smaller than you are.'

'We were going to let her have her turn,' said John, frowning. 'Mum, have the Healeys gone? The house looks quite empty.'

'Yes, they've gone,' said Mrs Carlton. 'The two old ladies were really too feeble to look after themselves any longer. So they have sold their house and gone to live with a niece. I went to say goodbye to them yesterday.'

'Who's coming to live in their house?' asked Marian. 'I hope it's a family with children.'

'Well, it is,' said Mrs Carlton. 'A family with four children. One is just a baby. The others are about your ages.'

'Oh!' said Marian, thrilled. 'We shall be able to make friends with them then. When are they coming?'

'Not till next week,' said Mrs Carlton. 'The house is being painted and cleaned first. I hope the new people will look after the garden a bit better than the old ladies did. Really, it is quite a disgrace.'

'Four children!' said John. 'I hope there's a boy for me.'

'And somebody for me,' said Annette. 'I want somebody to play with too. Don't I, Mummy?'

'Yes, dear,' said Mrs Carlton, putting her arm round small Annette. Annette was spoilt. She yelled when she couldn't get her own way. She sulked if she was scolded. She was pretty when she smiled and looked happy, but very ugly when she frowned or pouted.

'Marian and John always play together, and

8

they leave me out,' said Annette, cuddling up to her mother. 'I want somebody to play with too.'

'I only hope they'll be nice children,' said Mrs Carlton. 'I don't know anything about the family, except that they are called Taggerty. We'll have to wait and see what they're like.'

She went back to the house, taking Annette with her. Marian and John went on looking over the wall, jiggling the roller a little.

'Four children! That sounds good. Mum won't let us make friends with many of the children here – except those stuck-up Fitzgeralds, and they're boring. I hope they'll be fun, Marian!'

'John,' said Marian in a whisper, 'do you think we could slip over the wall and see the empty garden and peep in at the windows of the house? We've never been into this garden.'

John looked doubtful. 'Would it be all right?' he said. 'I mean – suppose somebody saw us?'

'Well, let's go this evening then, when there's nobody about,' said Marian. 'And don't tell Annette. We don't want her to come too. She'd only make a noise or something.'

'All right. We'll slip over the wall this evening,' said John. 'I've always wanted to explore the garden at the bottom of ours. I know it's all untidy and overgrown but it looks exciting and mysterious somehow, plenty of places to hide in, almost like a jungle.'

They heard their mother calling and slipped down from the roller. It was teatime. Annette was already sitting in her place, washed and brushed. Marian and John went to get themselves ready, too.

'You're late for tea,' said Annette, when they came back. 'I was first, Mummy. John hasn't washed his hands properly. I can see some black on them.'

John glared at Annette and put his hands under the table.

'Let me see your hands, John,' said Mrs Carlton. 'And don't glare at poor Annette like that. Oh, dear, you really must go and wash your hands properly. Are your hands clean, Marian?'

John left the table, still glaring. Annette took no notice at all, but helped herself to plenty of honey. Nobody said that Annette was a little tell-tale.

After tea, the children went out into the garden to play. John wouldn't play with Annette and she sulked.

'You're unkind to me! You're a horrid, sulky boy. Mummy said you were to play with me!' wailed Annette.

John took a hurried glance at the windows of the house. 'Be quiet, Annette! Don't make such

a noise. We'll play hide-and-seek if you like. You can find us when we call Cuckoo.'

Marian and John ran off, leaving Annette to count to a hundred before she came to find them. 'We'll hide at the back of the garden shed,' said John. 'She never thinks of looking there. We can keep away from her then. I'm cross with her. I shall be cross with her for two days.'

Marian knew he would, too. John remembered things too long. If anyone offended him or made him angry he thought about it for a long time, and wouldn't forgive them. He seldom flared up or quarrelled – he just said nothing, but went on thinking little

11

bitter thoughts that made him most unpleasant for some time.

They squeezed behind the shed. They had to push a bush out of the way first. It hid them nicely. They settled down in the small space there and whispered to one another.

'As soon as Annette goes to bed we'll hop over the wall. I do hope we shan't be caught.'

'We might find a window open, then we could go into the empty house,' John said daringly.

'The windows will all be shut,' said Marian. 'They always are in an empty house.'

'I'm coming,' yelled Annette, suddenly. 'Look out, I'm coming.'

She couldn't find them, of course. She hunted everywhere, and then burst into loud wails. 'Where are you? You're hiding away from me on purpose. Come out and let me find you.'

John and Marian knew they would have to come out or their mother would come running to see what was the matter with Annette. They came out of their hiding-place without being seen and jumped on Annette, who screamed in fright.

'Oh, don't! Where were you? I looked simply everywhere. I don't like hide-and-seek. Let's play something else.'

When Annette was called in to bed, the other two went down to the bottom of the garden.

They got up on the roller and then climbed to the top of the wall. John slid over first and then helped Marian. In a few seconds they were standing in the untidy garden, looking round in excitement.

'Come on. We'll go up this path. Look how the trees meet overhead.'

'And look at that funny old summerhouse! It's got trellis windows and a wooden seat running all the way round inside it! I wish we had one like that. We could play houses in it.'

They went up the path. Certainly the garden was very overgrown and neglected – but how exciting it was! There was a big tree that drooped long thin branches to the ground all round its trunk, so that under it was a big cave of green. It was a weeping willow, graceful and beautiful. The children pushed aside the drooping twigs and went into the green cave.

'Oh, it's lovely!' said Marian. 'John, I do hope we can make friends with the Taggerty children. It would be lovely to play here. And, oh look! There's a pond!'

So there was. Goldfish swam about in it and the water looked clear and cool. 'It would be nice to paddle there,' said Marian longingly.

'But Mum wouldn't ever let us,' said John. 'Look at the lawn, Marian. The grass is like a hayfield, and all the flowers in the bed are over-grown with weeds. What a shame!'

Both John and Marian were good little gar-deners. They had gardens of their own and kept them beautifully. Marian pointed to some fine rosebushes, unpruned but full of lovely roses.

'Look there! Did you ever see such roses! Oh, what a shame to let the garden go wild like this. I like the part at the bottom where it's all thick and green and mysterious – and I love that big cave-tree, with its long twigs drooping right down to the ground. But this bit would look much nicer if it was trim and neat.'

They went to the house. They peeped in at the kitchen window. It was empty and bare. A tiny mouse scuttled across the floor and Marian jumped.

'Oooh! A mouse! I'd hate to go inside there if mice are about.'

Marian was scared of mice and bats, moths and beetles, worms and earwigs. She was afraid of strange dogs, and hardly liked to stroke a cat in case it scratched her. The children had no pets, because their mother liked her house to be clean and spotless – and she said pets made it dirty and muddy, and covered everything with hairs.

They tiptoed to another window. They spoke in whispers, not because there was anyone to hear them, but because it was exciting.

There was no window open at all so they couldn't possibly get into the empty house, even if they wanted to – and Marian didn't want to, now that she had seen a mouse. Still, it was thrilling just peeping in.

The old ladies had left nothing in the house at all, except a pile of newspapers in a corner of the kitchen. One of the taps there dripped and the evening sun caught the drips and made them shine. Otherwise there was nothing to see.

A distant bell rang and John frowned. 'There's our bedtime bell. What a pity! We could have had a wonderful game under that cave-tree.'

'And we could play houses in that summer-house,' said Marian. 'John, the Taggertys aren't coming till next week. Let's creep over here each evening and play, till they come. The painters and cleaners will be gone then, and there will be no one to see us.'

'I don't think we really ought to,' said John, who was always rather afraid of doing anything that might not be quite right and proper, 'but we shan't be harming anyone. So let's!'

'Yes, let's!' said Marian thrilled. 'Come on, we must get back now without anyone seeing us. We'll come again tomorrow – but mind, not a word to Annette, or she'll tell.'

2

In the Other Garden

John and Marian couldn't help feeling that it was rather an exciting secret they had between them. They whispered about it, and Annette was cross because they stopped whenever she came near them.

'You might tell me,' she whined. 'You might! You've got a secret and you won't tell me. When I find out what it is – and I shall – I shall tell Mummy about it. Then you will wish you'd told me.'

'We might be whispering about your birthday,' said John. That made Annette look sweet again.

Marian and John waited impatiently for Annette to go to bed that night. As soon as she was called they ran down to the bottom of the garden. Marian had her best doll with her.

'I want to play houses with her in that summerhouse,' she said. 'You can be the father, I'll be the mother, and she's our child. What shall we call our house?'

'No, let's play caves in that big, drooping tree,' said John. 'We'll play that once we are inside that tree. We're absolutely safe. It will be our cave.'

'John, do you think we might pick one or two of those lovely red roses that are lost in the tangle of weeds?' asked Marian, when they were making their way through the overgrown bushes and trees.

'Well, they don't belong to us,' said John.

'I know. But do they belong to anybody just at present?' said Marian. 'They will bloom and fade and die – and nobody will enjoy them. I'd love to pick just two. I don't see that it would matter.'

'If everyone thought that, there wouldn't be a flower or a plant left in the gardens of empty houses,' said John. 'No, don't pick anything, Marian. We oughtn't to be here at all, really.'

They had a lovely game in the cave-tree. The light under the drooping, green-leaved twigs was green and cool and rather mysterious. It was fun to part the long, graceful branches and peer out into the bright evening sunshine.

'Any enemies about?' Marian would whisper.

'None,' John would whisper back. 'We can make a dash for the summerhouse!'

Then, pretending that enemies might be after them at any moment, the two would dash to the little summerhouse and fling themselves inside it.

Marian didn't like the summerhouse as much as she thought she would. She saw a spider run along the ceiling and it made her shiver. 'I'd like to clean this house from top to bottom,' she said. 'I'd chase away all the earwigs and spiders, and clean it nicely. Shall we bring some stuff and clean it tomorrow, John?'

'You can, if you like,' said John. 'I don't want to. I'd rather play in the cave-tree. I wish those Taggertys weren't coming for weeks. I do so like having this garden all to ourselves.'

'Well, it might be better fun when they do come,' said Marian, 'because if we make friends with them, they will let us come and play here – and six children could have a lot of fun together in that cave-tree and this summerhouse, and in that tangle of bushes and trees at the bottom, too. And what fun to have a pond to sail ships on. I wish we had one.'

The two children climbed over the wall the next evening. Then came the third. It was not so fine as it had been. When a few drops of rain fell, John pulled Marian under the cave-tree. It was quite dark there that evening, because there were big clouds low down in the sky, full of rain.

'We'll shelter here,' said John, in a whisper. 'I only hope Mum doesn't start calling us. But I think she's out now. This is a lovely cave, Marian. Not a drop of rain is getting through.'

He was right. The long, drooping branches waved to and fro a little in the wind, but no rain came through at all. The ground was perfectly dry to sit on. It was fun to sit there and hear the rain pattering outside.

Then suddenly the two children heard another noise. It was the sound of voices and hurrying feet. And the sound came from the back entrance of the house and garden!

John clutched Marian. 'It's somebody coming in here! I hope it isn't the Taggertys.'

Marian hardly dared to breathe. Her face went red and she sat absolutely still. The voices sounded very lively indeed, and the feet pattered to and fro.

'Bother this rain! What a pity, just when we wanted to see the house and garden in the sunshine. I say, look, there's a pond. Mummy, there's a pond!'

'John! We must go,' whispered Marian, in a panic. 'They'll find us here. Quick, let's go.'

'No, we'll be seen,' said John. He was frightened too. 'Oh, Marian, I wish you hadn't picked those two roses this evening!'

Marian wished she hadn't, too. It was the first time she had picked any of the flowers, but she had seen two perfect red roses and hadn't been able to stop herself from breaking them off. There they were, beside the trunk of the weeping willow. Where could she hide them?

There was nowhere. In despair, Marian sat her doll on top of them. There – now they wouldn't be seen.

'Pat! Look here! There's a wonderful garden shed,' cried a voice.

'Let's look at the garden. Goodness, Maureen, isn't it overgrown!' cried another voice. 'Blow this rain! Come on, we'll look all over the garden. It's a big one. Bigger than the ones we've had before. We'll have fun here.'

Another voice spoke – a younger, more childish voice. 'Take me, too! I want to come, too!'

'Say please, Biddy, then!' said Pat's voice. 'And don't whine like that.'

'Please!' said Biddy's voice, and then all the pattering feet came nearer.

'There's a summerhouse!' yelled Pat. 'Look! We can play houses and schools. And look at all these lovely trees to climb. I say – what's *this* tree?'

Marian and John clutched one another. They could see the toes of three children under the ends of the drooping willow branches. And then somebody parted the branches and looked inside.

It was a boy's face, a merry face with dark-blue eyes and dark curly hair. The boy was ten, just about John's age. He stared inside the cave-tree and saw Marian and John at once.

'Look, Maureen,' he said, startled, and pulled aside more branches for his sister to look inside the tree with him. 'Children! Hey, you, what are you doing here? This is *our* house and garden!'

Marian looked as if she was going to cry. John stood up. 'We only came in to have a look because the garden was empty,' he said. 'You're not living here yet. Don't tell your mother and father.'

'Why should we? We're not tell-tales!' said the boy, and came right inside the drooping ring of branches. 'But you just clear out, see? I won't have anyone in my garden without my permission.'

22

He looked very fierce. He also looked very dirty. His hands were black and he had a smear across his face. There was a hole in one of his socks and his jersey had a tear in it.

The girl came through the branches too. She was the same age as Marian, about eight. She too looked dirty and untidy. Then came a third child, about four. She was Biddy. She had the same blue eyes and dark hair of the other two, and she was just as untidy. Her red hair-ribbon was undone and trailed down her back.

'Where do you live?' demanded Pat.

'I shan't tell you,' said John, afraid that Pat might tell his father and mother. 'It's no business of yours. We've done no harm. We'll go.'

'No you won't! You're our prisoners!' Pat cried suddenly, and with a truly deafening yell he produced a rope from round his waist and rushed at John, meaning to tie him up.

John was not used to this sort of thing. He tried to push Pat away, but the boy soon got him on the ground, and Marian stared at them in horror.

'John! John! You'll dirty your jersey! Oh, John, get up!'

But then it was poor Marian's turn, for Maureen and Biddy suddenly flung themselves on her, too, and she also was rolled on the ground.

She screamed. What would Mother say to her dirty dress?

There was a real rough-and-tumble for a few minutes, and when it was over, John found that somehow or other his hands were tied behind his back. He was indeed Pat's prisoner.

'You beast!' he shouted to Pat. 'Undo my hands. I'll kick you if you don't.'

'Kicking not allowed,' said Pat. 'Don't be an ass. It's only a game.'

Marian sat up and dusted down her dress. It was in a dreadful mess. 'Don't dare to touch me again!' she yelled at Maureen and Biddy. 'Look what you've done to my dress! Mummy will be furious.'

'No harm done,' said Maureen, dimples coming in her cheek as she grinned at the angry Marian. 'A button off – but what does that matter?'

'What does that matter?' echoed Biddy, jumping up and down in glee at the sight of Marian's angry face. 'Oh look – there's a doll!'

'Let my doll alone!' screamed Marian, who was now quite beside herself with rage and fright. 'If you dare to touch her, I'll – I'll – I'll . . .'

But it was no use. Biddy had got the doll and was cuddling her. Then Pat saw the two red roses under the doll and he picked them up.

'Oho! You've been picking our roses,' said Pat. 'Haven't you?'

John and Marian were both truthful children. They had been taught never to tell lies, and they never did. But how dreadful to have to own up to picking somebody else's flowers!

'I picked them,' said Marian, at last. 'I didn't think it would matter. They were fading. I'm sorry now – I wouldn't have picked them if I'd known you were coming and might want them.'

'She's a thief,' said Biddy, importantly.

'Shut up, Biddy,' said Pat, at once. He turned to Marian. 'You'd no right to pick our flowers.

25

But you can have them. We'll take your doll in exchange.'

'No, oh no!' cried Marian. But Maureen was already running out of the willow tree with the doll. Marian tore after her.

A voice came from somewhere. 'Children! Do you want to see over the house? I've got the key now.'

Maureen flung the doll to Marian. 'Here you are. That's our mother. I was only teasing you.'

'Keep the roses too, if you're so badly off for flowers,' called Pat, in a scornful voice. He took Biddy's hand and they all ran to the house.

'What horrid, rough, unkind, dirty, *dreadful* children!' said Marian, almost in tears, as she picked up her doll and hugged her. 'I hate them.'

'Beasts,' said John, looking down at his dirty jersey. 'Springing on us suddenly like that and getting us down on the ground. I never knew such rough children in my life!'

'I don't want to know them,' said Marian. 'Come on, John, let's go while we can. They may come back at any minute.'

They peeped out between the willow branches. They saw a crowd of people in the empty house, and heard the sound of lively, excited voices.

'They had nice faces, those children,' said

26

Marian, remembering. 'Lovely blue eyes. But what awful manners! Mummy would hate them, I'm sure. She'd never let us know them. Anyway, I shall never, never be friends with them after what they did with my doll. Poor Angela! I thought she'd be ruined. Let's go home quickly, John.'

They ran hurriedly down the garden, and got over the wall. They heard their bedtime bell as they climbed over. John looked down at his clothes in dismay.

'Mum will have a lot to say,' he said. 'And you look pretty awful too, Marian.'

Mrs Carlton did have a lot to say. She couldn't bear the children to be dirty or untidy. 'Your jersey, John! Your dress, Marian! And where's that missing button? What *have* you been doing?'

They didn't tell her. They both thought the same thing: Those dreadful children! We'll never speak to them again!

3

The Taggertys move In

Neither Marian nor John dared to climb over the wall into the other garden again in the evenings. It had been a great shock to them to be caught like that by the Taggertys, and given such a rough time. They talked about it to one another when Annette wasn't there.

'We can't possibly be friends with them. They were so rough and dirty and horrid. The way they got us down like that!'

'Yes – and the way they took poor Angela and then threw her back, and made her fall on the ground,' said Marian. 'Thank goodness she was all right. I've never broken a doll in my life, and I simply couldn't bear it if Angela got hurt. Horrible children!'

'It's quite certain Mum will never let us know them,' said John, 'so that will be all right. I wonder when they will arrive.'

The Taggertys moved in one day the following week. John had to take a message from his mother to someone living two doors away from the Taggertys' house, and as he passed by he saw two big removal vans backing up to the front gate. They're moving in, he thought, and stood for a minute to watch. Some of the furniture was carried into the house as he watched. John thought it wasn't very nice furniture. It looked shabby and old, not like theirs at home, which was always fresh and shining and spotless.

A big, plump woman, with untidy hair and a loud voice, came out of the house. 'The next lot is to go into the room on the right,' she told the men, in a cheerful voice that could be heard all down the road. That must be Mrs Taggerty, thought John. She looks quite jolly, but isn't she untidy! Just like those dreadful children.

He wondered when the children would arrive. There was no sign of them then. Only Mrs Taggerty seemed to be there. Perhaps the children would arrive later. He went along to deliver his message and stayed for a while with his mother's friend, waiting while she wrote an answer for him to take.

Just as he passed the Taggertys' house a shabby old car drew up, and out of it tumbled three children. Yes, Pat, Maureen and Biddy. John saw another woman in the car, holding a big white bundle. That would be the baby. A man sat at the wheel, smiling. He had a long thin face, very deep-set blue eyes, and a mass of dark, wavy hair, grey at the edges. He looked nice. That must be Mr Taggerty, thought John, slipping quickly to the opposite side of the road so that the children wouldn't see him. He didn't mean to speak to them at all.

The children poured into the front garden, shouting in excitement, laughing in delight at coming to a new home. They didn't see John. Mrs Taggerty came to the front door and they flung themselves on her.

'Mummy! We've come at last! But what a pity, the vans got here first.'

'We had a puncture! It took ages to get the wheel off. We nearly went mad, it took so long.'

'I want to see the men putting the furniture into my bedroom. Have they done it yet? I want to tell them exactly where to put everything.'

Mixed up among the children's legs was a dog. It was a curious-looking dog, black and tan, with such a long tail that waved about like a plume. The dog was as excited as the children. It plunged about, barking madly. John didn't like the look of it at all.

What a dog! It's a terrible mongrel, he thought. It's not a terrier, or a spaniel, or a retriever – it's just a mix-up. And look at its awful tail! Well, I hope it never comes into our garden. If I catch it there, digging up our beds, I'll chase it out!

'Get down, Dopey, get down!' yelled Pat, as

the dog, trying to get the boy's attention, leaped right up at him and licked his face. 'Mum, Dopey was quite mad in the car. We had to open a window and let him put his head out all the time. Dad said he wanted to make sure we were taking the right road.'

'Woof,' said Dopey, in an excited doggy voice, and pawed at Mrs Taggerty.

'Good dog! Go indoors then!' said Mrs Taggerty. 'Patrick, try to keep him out of the men's way, or they'll be falling over him and dropping wardrobes down the stairs.'

Dopey disappeared into the house with a bound and a deep 'woof' and the children followed. The removal men went in with a dressing-table. Mr Taggerty got out of the car and helped the woman with the baby to the pavement.

'Come on, Bridget,' he said. 'We'll have to wake up Michael, I'm afraid. Well, what do you think of the house?'

John didn't want to hear or see any more. He sped home to tell Marian and Annette all about everything. He called them excitedly. 'Marian! Annette! I've got something to tell you.'

They listened eagerly to his story. Marian didn't at all like the sound of the big dog.

'I hope he doesn't come here. I should be afraid of him. Oh dear, I do wish the children were nice – it would be such fun to have three to play with, living just at the bottom of our garden.'

'How do you know they're not nice?' said Annette. 'You haven't even spoken to them.'

John and Marian didn't say they had. They knew Annette would go rushing to tell their mother if she knew they had been into the Taggertys' garden, and seen the children.

Mrs Carlton, too, heard that the Taggertys were moving in. 'I'll just wait and see what kind of people they are before I make friends with them, and go calling on Mrs Taggerty,' she said. 'Anyway, Mrs Wilson will know – the friend you took a message to this morning, John. She lives only two doors away and will be sure to know what they are like.'

'I didn't think they looked very nice when I passed by today,' said John. 'I saw the children going in. They were awfully noisy and excited.'

Although Marian and John had quite made up their minds not to speak to the Taggerty children any more, they couldn't help going down the garden to see if any of them were in their garden too.

Annette was standing on the garden roller, looking over the wall. From the other garden came the sound of shouts and calls, laughter, woofs and shrieks.

'They're in the garden,' said Annette.

'You needn't tell us *that*!' said John. 'We can hear.'

'I've seen the big dog,' said Annette. 'He's called Dopey. And they've got a big cat, too. I've seen it.'

'What's it like?' asked Marian.

'It's black, with four white feet and a white bib,' said Annette. 'And they call it Socks. Isn't that a silly name for a cat?'

'Yes, very,' said John. 'Socks! I suppose they call it that because it looks as if it's wearing white socks.'

'Socks and Dopey! What strange names for animals,' said Marian. 'Is Socks friendly with Dopey, Annette? Did you see?'

'Oh yes. Dopey chases Socks, and Socks chases Dopey,' said Annette. 'And when Socks is tired of being chased, she just runs up a tree. There she is now, look!'

The children looked. They saw a large black cat, with four white feet, sitting solemnly on the branch of a tree looking at them.

'Doesn't she look haughty?' said Marian. 'She looks as if she doesn't want to know us at all!'

'Well, look haughty back, then,' said John. 'We don't want to know her. Dreadful children, a silly dog and a haughty cat! Look out, here come the children. Let's hide.'

Pat, Maureen and Biddy appeared through the tangle of bushes at the bottom of their garden. Biddy was as black as a sweep, and her hair-ribbon was, as usual, undone, and trailed down her neck.

Marian and John ran to hide under a nearby bush. Annette wasn't quite quick enough. Pat saw her head above the wall just before she got down from the roller. He called to her.

'Hey, you! What's your name?'

Annette didn't answer. She scrambled down and fell off the roller, grazing her knee. At once she set up a terrific yell. Pat's head appeared above the wall.

'What's up? What a row!'

Annette pointed to her knee. The graze was so light that it could hardly be seen.

'Cry-baby!' said Pat. 'My little sister wouldn't howl for a graze like that!'

Annette was angry to hear herself called a cry-baby. 'Nasty boy!' she said. 'I'll tell my mummy you called me a cry-baby.'

'Dear little tell-tale!' said Pat, and grinned. 'Run away and tell her. Cry-baby! Tell-tale!'

Annette was so surprised and angry at this speech that she stood there with her mouth open, ready to howl, but quite forgetting to in her astonishment at hearing someone speaking to her so rudely and unkindly.

'If you don't close your mouth the flies will get in,' said Pat. 'Hey, Maureen, come on up here! There's a funny cry-baby over the wall with her mouth wide open.'

But before Maureen's head appeared, Annette was off up the garden to find her mother, screaming in anger. How dared that boy talk to her like that?

Mrs Carlton appeared at once and comforted her. 'Poor little Annette! Don't take any notice of such a rude boy! Did you hurt your poor knee? Why didn't John and Marian look after you?'

'They hid,' sobbed Annette. 'They don't look after me at all. They're horrid, too.'

'Now you choose a sweet out of the sweet-tin and go and play,' said Mrs Carlton. 'And don't go and look over the wall any more, in case those children are there. If that's the way they behave we won't have anything to do with them.'

4

Father's Little Surprise

Marian, John and Annette did keep away from the garden wall for the next two days. They heard the shouts of the Taggerty children, and they heard the deep woofs of Dopey. Once they heard the baby crying.

'I saw Pat looking over our wall this morning,' said John to Marian. 'I don't think we'd better let him see us because he doesn't know that we live here. He might go and tell Annette he saw us in his garden last week, if he sees us – and then she'd tell Mum.'

'I suppose Annette really is a tell-tale, just as Pat said,' said Marian. 'Fancy his telling her that! If we did, she'd complain to Mummy and we'd get a telling-off. Mummy always treats Annette as if she was still a darling baby, but she isn't. John, I wish I could see that baby next door. I do like babies. They're better than dolls because they can really move and make noises.'

'I don't want to see the baby!' said John, scornfully. 'It will be like the rest of them, dirty and rude, and smelly too, I expect.'

'Oh, I shouldn't like it very much if it was

smelly,' said Marian. 'I hope it isn't. I like the smell of babies usually, such a nice fresh baby-smell – baby powder and soap. I wonder if it's a boy or a girl.'

Mrs Carlton went to see her friend, Mrs Wilson, to ask her about the Taggertys. 'Are they nice?' she asked. 'What about the children? One of them wasn't very polite to little Annette the other day.'

'My dear, they're awful!' said Mrs Wilson, wrinkling up her nose. 'Not at all the sort of people for our road. A great pity they came, I think.'

'Oh, dear,' said Mrs Carlton. 'What a shame! As they live at the bottom of our garden I rather hoped they would be nice. The children would like to play with others living so near.'

'They've no manners at all,' said Mrs Wilson. 'Not one between them. *And* Mrs Taggerty

came borrowing something the very day after she moved in. And hasn't returned it yet. Such an untidy woman, too. Pleasant though. She had a dreadful dog with her that simply romped all over my geraniums. And Mrs Taggerty never said a word to stop him.'

'Oh, dear!' said Mrs Carlton again. 'I'm afraid they will be impossible as friends. I must warn the children to have nothing to do with them.'

'My dear, your three are so well brought up that I am sure they wouldn't have anything to do with the Taggertys anyhow,' said Mrs Wilson. 'That little Annette of yours now, a sweet child, with such lovely manners. What a pretty little thing she is, and you always dress her so beautifully, too.'

Mrs Carlton was pleased. 'Yes, Annette is a pet. Well, all of them are, really, though my husband does complain sometimes about them. He'd like them to swarm up trees and tear their clothes, and crawl through bushes and splash through puddles and goodness knows what. Well, there's no need for children to do things like that, and I don't like it. I like well-brought-up, well-behaved children, who like to be clean and tidy, and helpful to others.'

'Well, yours certainly are all that,' said Mrs Wilson. 'A pleasure to be with. Do let them come to tea with me one day next week. As for those Taggertys, don't you let your children mix with them. Yours might be good for the Taggertys, but the Taggertys wouldn't be good for *yours.*'

When Mrs Carlton got home she called the children to her. 'I'm sorry to say that I haven't had a very good report about the Taggertys,' she told them. 'There's no need to repeat to you what I've heard, but all I want to say is this – the Taggerty children are not our sort, and I don't want you to play with them. You can be polite and say hello, but no more than that.'

The children were glad. They didn't want to know those rough children and their dog.

'I don't expect they go to church and I don't expect they even say their prayers,' said Marian. 'Do you think they clean their teeth, Mummy?'

'Oh, I expect so,' said her mother. 'That's their business, not ours. Now, I'm going to go and see Granny. Who wants to come with me?'

Nothing more was said about the Taggertys that day. The three children spent the rest of the day with their grandmother, and she praised their behaviour to their mother.

'Really, they are a credit to you,' she said. 'You are lucky to have such good children. I don't believe they are ever naughty.'

'No, they're not really naughty,' said Mrs Carlton. 'Their father says sometimes he wishes they were. He thinks they're *too* good, you know. But that's only because he was a very naughty little boy when he was small, and he can't understand their not wanting to be naughty and mischievous, too.'

The children didn't go down to the bottom of the garden at all for some days. Annette wouldn't even go halfway down, she was so afraid of seeing Pat and having something rude called out to her. They couldn't help hearing the Taggerty children though, for they always seemed to be playing some exciting game.

'Cowboys and Indians, or Robbers and Policemen, I should think,' said John. 'I wish they were nice. I'd love to play those games with them. It's no fun playing them with Annette, because she screams at the least thing.'

Then on Saturday something surprising happened. It was when the children were having lunch. Mr Carlton carried in the casserole, and then began to talk.

'Alice,' he said, 'I met a very well-known writer yesterday. I meant to have told you. He was at school with me as a boy, and when he grew up he became famous as a writer of books. Very good books they are, too.'

'Really?' said Mrs Carlton, busy dishing up vegetables. 'Where did you meet him?'

'Well, I went to a tea shop I sometimes go to, to buy chocolates for you and the children,' said Mr Carlton, 'and there, having tea, was old Dickie – and his family with him! My word, you'd have liked his children, Alice.'

'What were they like?' asked Marian.

'Well, there was a boy, about John's age, I suppose,' said Mr Carlton. 'A nice boy, cheerful and with plenty to say. A good athlete too, won all the races at his last sports, can climb any tree, according to his father, and is as plucky as a boy can be. He broke his ankle last year, doing something mad, and never made a murmur about it.'

'What were the others like?' asked Annette.

'There was a girl like you, Annette, an amusing little thing. She was quite squashed by the others, but she didn't seem to mind a bit. A little monkey, I should think. And there was another girl, too. I liked her very much. So natural and friendly.'

'They sound nice,' said Marian.

'They were rather noisy and excited,' said Mr Carlton. 'Their mother was there too – such a nice, friendly woman, enjoying the treat as much as the children were. Well, well, it *was* a surprise to meet old Dickie, I must say – and to find him with a family too. Of course, I told him all about you – and I do want you all to be friends.'

'Oh yes!' said Annette. 'I want a friend. I'd like that little girl to play with. But where do they live, Daddy?'

'Well, now I've got a surprise for you,' said Mr Carlton, beaming all round the table. 'A real surprise. They've come to live here, in our village! They live next door but two to Mrs Wilson, Mummy's friend. Isn't that strange? It will be nice to have old Dickie round in the evenings.'

There was a silence. Everyone looked at Mr Carlton. Mrs Carlton asked the question they were all thinking. 'Peter – what is their name?'

'Taggerty,' said Mr Carlton. 'Dickie Taggerty sat by me at school, and he was always first in English and vowed he'd be a writer one day. And so he is – I am proud to know him. Well, you'll call on Mrs Taggerty, won't you, Alice, and ask the children round to tea?'

There was another silence. The children's hearts sank. Goodness! To think it was the Taggertys that their father had been talking about. That dreadful family.

'Oh dear,' said Mrs Carlton, at last. 'Peter, the Taggertys live in the house whose garden joins ours at the bottom. And, dear, they are not really very nice children. So rough and dirty and rude.'

'Well – they seemed a little untidy, and they certainly had plenty to say, and could have done with a little better manners,' said Mr Carlton, 'but they were thoroughly nice children, natural, jolly and friendly. I liked them. It would do ours good to know them. And it might do them good to know ours too. You'd like Mrs Taggerty, I'm sure, dear. Most amusing, and so friendly.'

Mrs Carlton didn't look as if she would like Mrs Taggerty. Whatever was she to do? She didn't want to make friends with the Taggertys at all – and now Mr Taggerty had turned out to be her husband's old friend at school! It really was too bad.

'Well, will you call on the Taggertys?' asked Mr Carlton, sounding a little impatient. 'I want to ask old Dickie round here, and we must ask his wife too. And the children would mix quite well together – exactly the right ages. There's a baby too, Mrs Taggerty said.'

'I don't think they would mix, Peter,' said Mrs Carlton. 'Really, the Taggerty children are very rough and not well brought up at all. I don't want John and Marian to make friends with children like that.'

'John's too careful,' said Mr Carlton. 'I want him to be more of a boy. That elder Taggerty boy will shake him up a bit. And the little girl will soon stand up to Annette and teach her not to cry so much.'

John looked alarmed, and Annette looked ready to cry. Mr Carlton looked at Marian.

'And I've no doubt Marian will get over her fear of this, that and the other,' he said. 'The Taggerty children have all kinds of pets – a dog, a cat, pet mice—'

Marian gave a scream. 'Mice! I'll never never go near the Taggertys if they keep mice.'

'I had twenty pet mice once,' said her father, 'and two of them lived in my trouser-pocket for a week. It's a pity you children have no pets. You none of you seems to have my love for animals. I'd like a dog myself, but I suppose

Marian and Annette would have a fit if it jumped up at them. Alice, it's time we did something about these children of ours. They're good and well-behaved, and truthful, and nice-mannered – but are they *real* children? No, they're not! I tell you, they want a bit of shaking up.'

'I don't agree with you, Peter,' said Mrs Carlton, in a smooth sort of voice. 'But don't let's discuss it now, dear. I will call on Mrs Taggerty, if you want me to, but please don't make us enter into any close friendship with them, if we do find they are not the kind of people we like.'

'Well, we'll see,' said Mr Carlton, looking rather annoyed. 'What's the pudding? Oh, cherry pie, good! I'll have a nice big helping, please, because I'm going for a long walk this afternoon. Anyone want to come with me?'

Nobody did. John knew he ought to say he would come, because his father liked boys who wanted to go for long walks and tramp through the woods and over the hills. But John didn't like walks. He wanted to stay at home and read.

'Well, I'm off,' said Mr Carlton, in a disappointed voice, when he had finished his pie. 'Now, if only we had a dog I could take him for company. But we haven't. Goodbye.'

5

Over the Wall

The children felt very gloomy after their father had gone. They went upstairs and talked about things.

'Isn't it bad luck?' said John. 'To have to know those dreadful children. And how mean of Dad to say I'm too careful. I'm not, am I?'

'Well – you don't climb trees or anything,' said Marian. 'Of course, Mummy doesn't like us to. So you can't very well help it.'

'It will be awful having those children here to tea,' said John. 'You'll have to put away your best dolls, Marian. That girl called Maureen will probably throw them about.'

'And you'd better put away your new aeroplane,' said Marian. 'You never know what children like that will do with other people's toys. I bet they haven't a single unbroken toy!'

'I hope they won't bring that dog here,' said Annette. 'I shall hit him if they do.'

'He'll bite you, then,' said Marian. 'He'll show his teeth – like this – and he'll growl – like this, grrrrrr.'

Annette screwed up her face to howl. 'It's all

right,' John said hurriedly. 'Marian doesn't really mean it. I'll see the dog doesn't bite you. We'll send it away if it comes.'

'I do hope Mummy doesn't ask them to tea,' said Marian. 'Perhaps she won't. Good gracious, can you hear those children playing now? What a noise they are making!'

It was rather an exciting noise. It sounded as if a big drum was being beaten. *Boom-boom-boom, diddy-boom-boom-boom!* Then there came what sounded like a trumpet noise.

'They're being a band, or something,' said John. 'Let's go down and see.'

They went downstairs and out of the back door to the bottom of the garden. Yes, there was certainly a drum all right. *Boom-boom-boom, diddy-boom-boom-boom.*

John couldn't resist putting his head over the wall. He saw Maureen, dressed up in a flowing red cloak, with a crown on her head, parading through the bushes. Behind her came Pat, banging a drum, and Biddy, blowing on a small trumpet.

'Here comes Her Majesty!' shouted Pat, banging the drum. 'Fall down before her!'

An angry voice came through the trees, and then someone appeared in a hurry. It was Bridget, their mother's help.

'Och, you naughty little ragamuffins, you,

making all that din with the baby, bless his heart, just asleep after a bad tummyache. One more beat of that drum, Patrick, and I'll take the stick from you and lay it about you till you boom like a drum yourself!'

The beating of the drum stopped at once. 'Oh, sorry, Bridget,' said Pat. 'I quite forgot about Michael. We'll play Cowboys and Indians instead.'

'Indeed you won't, not till the baby's awake and happy,' said Bridget. 'War-whoops and what-nots, and dancing round like mad things,

49

scaring the baby into fits. And your mother with a headache, too!'

She turned and went. John ducked his head down, for he didn't want to be seen. All was quiet for a few minutes, but then some other game started which had a lot of yelling in it.

'Aren't they awful?' said Marian. 'Their baby is asleep and their mother has a headache – and still they can't be quiet. Most selfish children!'

'I'd like to have seen Bridget take the drumstick and beat Pat like a drum,' said John.

On the next Tuesday, Mrs Carlton went to call on Mrs Taggerty. The children waited eagerly for her to come back.

They met her at their front gate. 'Mummy! What happened? Were all the children there? How did they behave?'

'I *suppose* they were on their best behaviour,' said Mrs Carlton. 'But I should be very sorry to think that any of you would behave as they do. Still, I suppose they can't help it. They've just been brought up like that. Mrs Taggerty is rather easy-going. The baby is lovely.'

'I'd like to see the baby,' said Marian. 'I do so like babies. Mummy, did you ask the Taggertys to tea?'

'Yes,' said Mrs Carlton. 'They are coming tomorrow. By themselves, without their mother.

She says Bridget is out tomorrow, and she must stay with the baby. So the children will come alone, at half past three. I do hope you will all get on together nicely.'

Marian, John and Annette looked gloomy. 'Mummy, will you be with us all the time?' asked Annette. 'I'm afraid of Pat.'

'No, I can't be with you all the time,' said her mother. 'You must play in the garden by yourselves before tea, but I shall have tea with you, of course. And after tea I might have a game of snap or something with you.'

That evening, when Annette had gone to bed, Marian and John heard someone whistling at the bottom of the garden. They went down cautiously to see who it was.

Pat's head stuck over the top of the wall. He beckoned to them. But when they came near he looked most astonished. 'I say! So *you* are the children we caught here! I didn't know you lived over the wall. Did you know we were coming to tea with you tomorrow?'

'Yes,' said John. 'Don't go and say anything about us being in your garden. We'll get into a row if you do.'

Pat made a scornful noise. 'Tell tales about you! What do you think I am? I wouldn't dream of saying a word. Gosh, fancy it being *you* we're coming to tea with. I say, your mother came to

51

call on ours this afternoon, and she was so awfully polite and well-dressed and – er – er – well, stuck-up a bit, you know, that we got quite scared. So we thought we'd whistle you tonight, and see what you were like. We hoped you wouldn't be stuck-up too. We can't bear stuck-up people.'

'Mum isn't stuck-up,' said John stiffly.

'Well, we've heard people say she is,' said Maureen, her head popping up beside Pat's. 'I thought she was awfully pretty and I did like her dress. People say you children are rather awful too. Are you? Harry Lee told us you were prigs.'

Marian wasn't sure what a prig was, but it sounded something horrid. She went red. John looked sulky.

'We're not prigs. People think you're pretty awful too. And so you are. We don't want you to come to tea a bit.'

'And we don't want to come,' said Maureen, her eyes shining angrily. 'Horrible, having to dress up and come in all polite and silly. And we shan't play any decent games, I bet, or climb a tree. Just sit around and make polite conversation like your mother does.'

'You're very rude,' said John. 'If it wasn't for our fathers knowing each other we wouldn't have to know you at all. We think you're an awful lot of children.'

'We think the same about you,' said Pat, his eyes shining angrily now too. 'That's what we call you – those dreadful children.'

'Oh – it's exactly what we call *you*,' said John, surprised. 'Well, don't come to tea if it's such a frightful bore.'

'We shall jolly well have to,' said Pat, gloomily. Then he brightened a little. 'We might say we feel ill,' he said, turning to Maureen. 'Do you remember how we got out of going to see that great-aunt of ours once? We both said we had awful sore throats, and Mum got alarmed and wouldn't let us stir out of the house.'

John and Marian were really shocked. 'But that was a terrible lie,' said Marian. 'Do you really tell lies like that? We never do.'

'Our father says it's a cowardly thing to do, to tell lies,' said John. 'He says people only tell them when they're too afraid to tell the truth. He says it's better to tell the truth and take what's coming to you than tell a lie to get out of it, because if you keep doing that you'll always be a coward, and wriggle out of things.'

Pat and Maureen stared at him in silence. 'We're not cowards,' said Pat at last. 'I can climb higher than any boy I know, and I can swim as fast as Dad. Maureen's brave too.'

'All the same, you are cowards if you keep on telling lies,' said Marian. 'You ask your father and see what he says. Now if *we* didn't want to come to tea with you – which we don't, of course – we wouldn't be cowardly and go and tell our mother we'd got sore throats and worry her to death – we'd be brave and go and say we jolly well didn't want to, and why. See?'

'I bet you wouldn't!' said Pat, scornfully. 'You'd just say, "Yes, Mother dear," and come. Pooh! I bet you're all three of you little cowardy-custards.'

A bell rang. 'That's our bell,' said Marian, thankfully, for she didn't want to argue with Pat any more. 'Well, I suppose we'll have to see you tomorrow.'

'Wait a bit,' said Maureen, urgently. 'We wanted to ask you something. We know our father wants us to be friends with you because he likes yours so much – and we don't want to let him down if we can help it. So for goodness sake tell us what to wear, and does your mother like to shake hands with us, or is she the kissy sort?'

'She won't want to kiss *you*,' said John. 'Wear what you like. We don't care! But if you want our mother to think anything of you, come with clean hands and faces, and don't shout at one another, or push one another like you do.'

Maureen sighed. 'It's going to be awful,' she said. 'All right, we'll do our best. Only for

Daddy's sake though! I don't expect our mothers will like each other any more than *we* do – but Daddy likes to think we're all friends together, so that he can have your father in whenever he likes.'

'We must go,' said John, as the bell rang again more urgently. 'That's Mum ringing for us.'

'I say! Wait! There's one more thing,' called Maureen. 'We can bring Dopey, can't we?'

Marian and John stopped in their run back to the house and turned shocked faces to Pat and Maureen. 'What, bring that awful mongrel!' cried John. 'Of course not! Mum would have a fit.'

'But he *always* goes with us *everywhere*,' said Maureen. 'And he isn't an awful mongrel. He's the best dog in the world. He'll be heartbroken if he doesn't come with us. He'll bark the place down and keep Baby awake.'

'Let him!' said John, hard-heartedly. 'I tell you, Mum will send him home if he does come, and Annette will scream till she's blue in the face.'

'Does she really go blue in the face?' asked Maureen, with interest. 'I should like to—'

But, as the bedtime bell was rung impatiently for the third time, John and Marian fled at top speed down the trimly kept path to their house. Pat and Maureen gazed after them.

'What frightful kids! Goody-goody and namby-pamby and priggy-wiggy. I wish we hadn't got to go to tea with them tomorrow. I liked their father awfully, didn't you, when we saw him at the tea shop? I thought he must have really decent children.'

'So did I. But you can never tell,' said Maureen. 'Anyway, we've got to go tomorrow, and do let's try to look tidy and clean, for Daddy's sake. I hope I've got a clean frock. I bet Biddy hasn't. She gets dirtier than any of us.'

'Oh, well. Tomorrow won't last for ever,' said Pat, as they went indoors. 'But just fancy having to go out to tea with those dreadful children.'

6

The Taggertys come to Tea

Six children felt very gloomy the next day, and wished heartily that something would happen to stop the tea party. But nothing did. The weather was fine. Everyone was quite well. And half past three came nearer and nearer.

'Now are you clean and tidy, and ready for your visitors?' asked Mrs Carlton, coming upstairs. 'Let me see your hands, John. And your nails? Annette, I must brush your hair again.'

'But, Mum – the Taggertys won't care a bit if we're clean or dirty,' said John, impatiently. 'They'd *prefer* us dirty.'

'I'm not thinking what they like, but of what *I* like, and of what is right and proper,' said Mrs Carlton. 'And don't talk in that tone of voice, John. There, Annette! You look very sweet with that big blue bow. Now you'll be very nice with little Biddy, won't you? She may be shy at first.'

Marian felt quite certain that Biddy wouldn't be at all shy, but she didn't tell Annette so. She couldn't help wondering how the spoilt little Annette would get on with Biddy.

'There are the Taggertys now,' said Mrs

Carlton, hearing the front-door bell ring. 'You can choose some toys to take out into the garden.'

John wanted to say that he was sure the Taggertys would rather play catch or hide-and-seek – but he was certain his mother would forbid that, seeing that they were all dressed-up and clean. So he said nothing.

In came the Taggertys. They were clean, except that Biddy's knees looked as if she'd been crawling for half a mile on them in some muddy place. Their hair was brushed, and Biddy's ribbon, for once in a while, was done up. They had forgotten to see if their nails were clean, and not one of them had clean shoes.

Still, they had clean clothes on, and clean socks, and they advanced on Mrs Carlton politely, holding out their hands.

'How do you do?' said Mrs Carlton, smiling.

'Quite well, thank you,' said all the Taggertys in chorus. They had evidently been practising this. John then advanced and held out his hand, too.

'Goodness! Do we have to do it to you?' said Maureen, surprised. 'How silly!'

'Well, you needn't,' said John, suddenly feeling that it was silly, too. But Annette wanted to. She loved showing off her manners in front of others. People so often praised her for them in public. So she went forward and held out her hand to Biddy.

But Biddy put her hands behind her and stared. 'Hello!' she said. 'Are all these your toys?'

Then the Taggertys forgot any further politenesses and began to examine all the toys with close attention.

'Look at this! Is it a musical box? Play it for us.'

'What's this? It's a toy garage! Look at all the cars in it. Let's take them out.'

'Oh, Biddy! See this doll's-house! It's what we've always longed for. Marian, let's take all the furniture out!'

'I think it would be better if you all went to play in the garden this sunny afternoon,' said Mrs Carlton, seeing Marian's black looks at the thought of her doll's-house being emptied.

'Well, we'll take the doll's-house then – and the garage – and the musical box – oh, what lovely toys you've got!' cried Maureen. 'And let's take this baby doll, too.'

'No, you can't. She's mine,' said Annette.

'Well, we're visitors. You have to let us play with your things,' said Biddy. 'I want to carry this doll.'

'Shut up, Biddy,' said Pat. 'Don't talk like that.'

Annette snatched the doll away from Biddy. 'It's mine! I won't let you have it. Mummy, she's not to have my baby doll, is she?'

'Let Biddy carry it down to the garden,' said Mrs Carlton. 'She is your visitor, you know.'

Annette burst into tears.

'Cry-baby!' said Biddy at once. 'Isn't she, Pat? You told me she was, and she is! I don't want your silly doll, Annette. Cry-baby!'

'Now, don't quarrel,' said Mrs Carlton. 'Oh dear, there's the telephone. Take the Taggertys down to the garden, John, and look after them till teatime.' And with that Mrs Carlton went out of the room.

Annette felt hurt and cross. Her mother hadn't comforted her and fussed her as she usually did. She whimpered, feeling sorry for herself.

'Come on. Let's leave the cry-baby by herself,' said Maureen. 'Help me to carry this doll's-house down the stairs, Pat. Oh, I never saw such a beauty in my life.'

'Haven't you got one?' asked Marian, feeling pleased at this admission. 'Oh, do be careful not to tilt it. All the furniture slides about if you do.'

'We've got an old one belonging to Granny,' said Maureen. 'But everything in it is broken now. It's not much fun to play with because none of the furniture stands up properly. The legs are broken, you see.'

The doll's-house and the toy garage with the cars were taken down into the garden. No sooner had they got there and settled down on the grass than there came a scampering of feet, and up the path from the bottom of the garden tore Dopey, his long, lanky body wriggling in delight to see the three children he loved. He rolled over on his back in a ridiculous way and threw all his legs in the air, working them about vigorously.

'Woof!' he said. 'Woof!'

'Look – when he lies on his back and works his legs like that, we say he's riding a bicycle,' Pat said, and gave the delighted Dopey a prod in the tummy. 'Idiotic dog!'

Annette and Marian squealed in fright as the big dog came up and flung himself down beside them. They jumped up in horror. 'Send him away!'

'Why?' said Pat. 'He won't do any harm. He won't really. He's an awfully stupid dog – that's why we call him Dopey – but he's loving and harmless and he loves a game. Let him stay.'

Dopey rolled over on his side and found his head near John's knee. He put out a great pink tongue and gave John a wet lick on his arm. And John liked it.

'I don't mind him staying,' said John, and Marian and Annette stared at him in horror.

'He's got to go,' said Marian, beginning to tremble. 'I'm afraid of dogs. You know I am.'

'Cowardy-custard!' said Pat scornfully. 'Hi, Dopey. Lick her then!'

Dopey leaped up, ran to Marian, and gave her a great big lick on her bare arm. She squealed.

'Oh, how horrible! What a licky dog!'

'All dogs are licky,' said Pat. 'Lie down, Dopey, or you'll go home.'

'Woof,' Dopey said, and lay down most obediently. But he was up again in a second and playfully ran at Annette's bare legs. She gave such an agonized scream that her mother came running down the garden at once.

'Annette, darling, what *is* the matter?'

Annette flung herself on her mother. 'Mummy, it's that dog! He rushed at me. He'll bite me.'

Mrs Carlton eyed Dopey, who laid himself flat on the ground and then squirmed towards her on his tummy, putting himself down most humbly. She gave him a very cold look.

'Is this your dog?' she said to Pat. 'Well, you must take him home. I'd rather he didn't come into our garden.'

'I want him here,' said Biddy, in a piercing voice.

'Biddy! I'll take you home too if you butt in like that,' roared Pat, making everyone jump. Biddy said no more. Pat got up. He was evidently still on his best behaviour.

'I'll take him back home,' he said, and went off down the side path to the front gate. He took Dopey home and pushed him into the garden shed. He shut the door on him and Dopey howled.

When Pat got back, the others were playing with the garage and the doll's-house, and for a while all was peace. But suddenly there came the scampering of feet again, and up from the

bottom of the garden gambolled Dopey, looking very pleased with himself indeed. Somebody had opened the shed door, he had run to the wall, leaped right over it – and here he was, overcome with delight at his own cleverness. He lay on his back and did his bicycle act again.

'He's awfully good at that,' said John, who was beginning to feel quite warmly towards this peculiar dog.

Dopey gave John a sudden slobbering lick. John patted his head. Marian watched in surprise. 'Don't let him come near me,' she said. 'I don't like him. He's so floppy and clumsy.'

'I'm going to tell Mummy,' Annette said, and got up. 'Nasty, horrid dog! I'm going to tell Mummy.'

'No, you're not,' said Pat, unexpectedly, and he took hold of her dress. 'Sit down, tell-tale. Do you know what you want? You yell just for nothing, and what you want is something to make you yell. If I were John I'd slap you every time you told tales or yelled. That's what we do to Biddy.'

Annette was so shocked at this surprising speech that she couldn't even yell.

'Look at her,' said Pat, to the others. 'Mouth wide open again, ready to yell. Flies will get into it, cry-baby! Look out, there comes a bee! He's looking for a hole!'

Annette heard the bee and shut her mouth with a snap. Dopey flopped down on her feet, and she freed a foot and kicked him.

In an instant Pat was standing beside her, his face red with anger. 'If I wasn't a visitor I'd give you such a slap for that that you'd never forget it,' he said. 'What's John doing, that he doesn't make you behave? You're a spoilt little girl, that's what you are. Kicking a dog! When he wants to make friends with you, too. Coward!'

'Don't! Don't!' begged Annette, really frightened at being spoken to like this. 'I won't do it again. John, tell him I didn't mean it.'

But John too had been shocked at seeing Annette kick Dopey. 'You *did* mean it,' he said. 'Sit down and behave yourself, Annette. We're all ashamed of you.'

Annette looked as if she was going to yell, but, seeing five pairs of stern eyes on her, she suddenly sat down. She said nothing more. John and Marian looked at one another. It was the very first time Annette had ever been known to do something she didn't really want to do.

'Do you think I'd better take Dopey back home again?' asked Pat, in his ordinary voice. He seemed to have forgotten his sudden anger completely. 'Blow you, Dopey. I'll be spending all the afternoon trotting you home!'

Everyone laughed except Annette, who still looked very solemn. Dopey gave a little whine and put his head on John's knee.

'He likes John,' said Pat. 'Look at him. He doesn't do that to everyone.'

John felt terribly pleased. He patted Dopey's silky head again. Dopey licked him slavishly and rolled his eyes in a most comical manner. He really was a peculiar dog, but John couldn't help liking him.

And when Mrs Carlton came to see how they were all getting on, there was Dopey again, flopping his long length on the grass with the six children. Mrs Carlton didn't say a word. As for Dopey, he looked away and pretended he wasn't really there. He wasn't such a stupid dog as he looked!

7

Teatime and After

Things went very well until five minutes before tea. Then the Taggertys got tired of sitting about and proposed a game of hide-and-seek. In three minutes all of them were dirty and Biddy had lost her ribbon and torn her frock.

Pat had climbed a tree and got the seat of his shorts stained with black. Maureen had squeezed behind a big oil-can in the garage and had oil on her skirt and hands. John, excited by the game, had actually got dirty too and even Marian and Annette were not clean and tidy.

Dopey had gone quite mad over the game. He floundered about all over the place, and his big footmarks were all across the rose-beds under the dining-room windows. Then he sat down on some snapdragons to scratch himself, and broke them to bits.

'Look at him!' cried Annette. 'What will Mummy say? He's a bad dog.'

'He doesn't mean to be,' said Maureen. 'He really has behaved awfully well, for him. Is that the tea-bell? I'm hungry.'

Mrs Carlton couldn't help exclaiming in

horror when she saw them. 'How have you got like that? Oh dear, John, take them to wash. I must mend your frock, Biddy. And what have you got all down that skirt, Maureen?'

'Have we really got to go and wash all over again?' said Pat, in dismay. 'We've already washed once this afternoon, before we came here. Can't we have a picnic tea in the garden, Mrs Carlton? I'll help to carry things out. It won't matter how dirty we are then.'

'No,' said Mrs Carlton, rather stiffly. 'Tea is laid in the house. Hurry and wash now.'

Grumbling under his breath, Pat went to wash with the others. Dopey came bounding along too, but Mrs Carlton shooed him out and shut the back door on him. He sat outside and howled dismally. It was a dreadful sound. The Taggertys were upset.

'Dopey's feet are clean, John. Why can't he come in? Doesn't your mother like dogs? Your father does. He told us so.'

Dopey had to sit outside all the time they had tea. He howled without stopping and Mrs Carlton felt very cross. Dreadful dog!

The Taggertys were very hungry, for they had had an early lunch as Bridget had wanted to go out to catch the half past one bus. They looked at the plates of bread-and-butter and cakes.

The bread-and-butter was cut very thin. At

home the Taggertys had thick slices. Goodness – six of these would only make one of the home slices. Mrs Carlton would think them very greedy if they ate all they wanted.

She did think them greedy. They really had no manners at all at the table. They never passed each other anything. They didn't wait to be asked to take this or that, they just stretched out and took it. They didn't say please and they didn't say thank you. They were certainly not at their best at meals. The buns were small. The slices of cake were only half the size of the ones they had at home. The Taggertys, afraid that they wouldn't have enough to eat, ate swiftly and silently. Outside Dopey howled and howled.

How dreadful they are, thought Mrs Carlton. Why weren't they taught their manners? Such good looking children too. Then she spoke aloud. 'No, no, Biddy. Don't snatch the last cake off the plate like that. See if somebody else wants it first.'

'I want it,' said Annette, at once.

'You would!' said Pat. 'Give it to her, Biddy.'

'No,' said Biddy, and held on to it.

'GIVE IT TO HER,' roared Pat, making everyone jump. Biddy gave the cake to Annette. Pat looked round the table. 'That's the way to treat them when they're spoilt,' he said. 'That's how you ought to treat Annette, John. Yell at her a bit. She'll soon grow a lot more sensible! What's the good of being an older brother or sister if you don't teach the young ones how to behave?'

'John has been taught to treat his little sister politely and kindly,' said Mrs Carlton, sharply. Pat stared at her.

'Well,' he said, trying to find words that would not offend his hostess, 'well – look what's happened! She's a screamer and a tell-tale.'

Annette wept. 'Don't be so unkind,' said her mother, and put her arm round Annette. 'Don't take any notice of him, dear. He doesn't know any better.'

Pat looked uncomfortable. 'I'm sorry,' he

said. 'I shouldn't have said that. I didn't know how to say it without offending you, Mrs Carlton. I'm very sorry.'

'It's all right,' said Mrs Carlton. 'Now stop crying, Annette. You don't want to make your pretty face ugly.'

'Is she pretty?' said Biddy, looking hard at Annette. 'I didn't think she was.'

'Nor are you,' said Pat at once. 'Have we all finished? Can we go now, Mrs Carlton?'

They all went off into the garden. Really! thought Mrs Carlton, as she looked out of the window and saw Dopey, mad with joy, careering round them all again. Really! I never came across such children in my life. Never!

She let them play for half an hour and then called them in. 'Would you like a game of snap? I'll have one with you, if you like.'

The Taggerty children would much rather have played out of doors. 'Can Dopey come with us, then?' asked Maureen. 'He'll only howl if he doesn't.'

'Oh, very well,' said Mrs Carlton, feeling that she would allow anything rather than have the dismal howling again. 'Or no – I know what we'll do. We'll take the cards out of doors and play on the grass. Then Dopey can be with you, and perhaps he'll be quiet and behave himself.'

Soon they were all playing snap. But as usual,

Mrs Carlton let Annette have the cards when she really shouldn't have had them. 'You don't mind, do you?' she said to Pat and Maureen. 'She's so small, you see. She gets upset if she doesn't win a few times.'

Nobody said anything to that. Pat looked sharply at Biddy, as if he wondered whether she, too, would expect to take cards when she hadn't really said 'Snap' first.

Soon Mrs Carlton handed some cards to Biddy that really she herself had won. 'You have these,' she said.

'But I wasn't first in saying "Snap",' said Biddy. 'You were!'

'Never mind. You've only two left. You can have these,' said Mrs Carlton.

'But isn't that cheating?' said Biddy. 'Pat says it is. And anyway I'm not a baby like Annette. I shan't cry if I don't get the cards. I'd rather not have them, Mrs Carlton. I like to play our way. Annette can play your way.'

Mrs Carlton was astonished. After that, nobody had any cards given to them that they hadn't really snapped. Pat won the game. He was very sharp indeed, much sharper than John.

'Now what about a game of snakes and ladders,' said Mrs Carlton. 'We've got two boards.'

'I'm tired of sitting still,' said Pat. 'Can't we run about again? What about Indians? Dopey's awfully good at Indians, John. He can wriggle along on his tummy just like we can.'

John was filled with admiration. 'Tell him to, then.'

'He won't, unless we're all doing it,' said Pat. 'Hey, Dopey! Indians. Shhh! Enemies ahead!'

He flopped down on his tummy, and so did Maureen and Biddy. They wormed their way along on the grass and Dopey did exactly the same. John shrieked with laughter, and even Marian smiled to see him.

'Your clothes!' said Mrs Carlton, in despair. 'No, John, don't you wriggle too. What will your mother say to your dress when you get home, Maureen?'

'Well, she did say it would be more sensible to put on old things to come and play,' said Maureen. 'But we knew you wanted us to be polite. Oh – here's Uncle Peter!'

Mr Carlton came into the garden, beaming. He had come home early on purpose to see the Taggertys before they went home. They greeted him as if he was indeed a real uncle.

'You've come in time to see us! Look, Dopey knows you again!'

'Will you give me a piggyback?'

'Uncle Peter, would you like to see me climb a tree?'

Dopey leaped up at Mr Carlton and gave him

a lick on the nose. Mr Carlton patted him and tickled him behind the ears. Dopey went nearly mad with joy.

Soon Mr Carlton was galloping round the garden with Biddy squealing on his back. Maureen ran after him, whipping him with a little twig. Pat shinned up a tree and yelled to him. 'Here I am! Did you see me get up?'

Dopey galloped round madly, running over the beds and making Mrs Carlton feel that he really was doing it on purpose. John, Marian and Annette watched all this half jealously. They

didn't like sharing their father with the Taggertys. And how those Taggertys liked him!

'It's time you went home, youngsters,' said Mr Carlton at last. 'I'll pop you over the wall, and come over with you myself to have a few words with your father.'

'Oh, not over the wall!' said Mrs Carlton.

'Well, they're too dirty now to walk round home by the road,' said Mr Carlton, reasonably. 'We won't be a minute.'

The Taggertys and Mr Carlton went off down the garden, talking nineteen to the dozen. Dopey followed them, barking.

'Well! Not a word of thanks! Not even a goodbye,' said Mrs Carlton. 'What badly-brought-up children.'

'I don't want them again,' said Annette. 'Pat was unkind to me. And I don't like Biddy. I don't want her for a friend.'

'Clear up everything,' said Mrs Carlton. 'Then you must go to bed, Annette. It's past your bedtime.'

In twenty minutes' time, Mr Carlton came back. And dear me, with him were the three Taggertys, still dirty and untidy, and all looking rather ashamed of themselves.

'Please, Mrs Carlton,' said Pat, 'we forgot to thank you very much for having us and to say goodbye. So we've come back to apologise.

Mum did tell us to be sure and thank you. I can't think how we forgot. I suppose it was because we went off with Mr Carlton like that.'

'Thank you very much for having us,' said Maureen.

'And for the nice tea,' said Biddy.

'And please can John and Marian and Annette come to tea tomorrow?' said Pat.

'Isn't that nice!' said Mr Carlton, in a hearty sort of voice. 'Of course they'll come, Pat. Now, off you go, Taggertys. Want a leg-up over the wall?'

'Goodbye,' Mrs Carlton said faintly. The Taggertys were really too much for her.

'Goodbye!' yelled John – suddenly feeling pleased at the invitation to tea. 'Tell Dopey I'll see him tomorrow. Goodbye!'

He went down the garden a little way after the departing guests. Pat slipped back to him. 'I say,' he said, 'isn't your father great? He's wizard! I wish mine was as much fun as that – but he's the quiet sort. I do really like your father awfully.'

John felt a glow of pride. He grinned at Pat. 'He's not a bad sort,' he said. 'I'm glad you like him. Well, see you tomorrow. Tell Dopey to behave himself till I come.'

8

Visiting the Taggertys

The next morning Pat popped his head over the wall when he heard John playing with Marian.

'I say! My mother says will you put on your oldest clothes, please, when you come this afternoon, and we can really play some exciting games? Come early. Can't you come at three?'

John's eyes shone. Exciting games! Would that mean Cowboys and Indians – and crawling on his tummy, with Dopey crawling beside him? That would be fun.

'Yes, we'll put on old clothes,' he said. 'And we'll come at three. That's if Mum lets us.'

'We're going to have a picnic tea under the weeping willow,' said Pat. 'Don't you think that's an exciting sort of tree, John? It's like a big, round, green cave. We play that it's our home and we're quite safe there.'

'That's what Marian and I said, when we came over into your garden before you moved in,' said John.

Annette and Marian were not so keen as John on putting on old clothes. Annette loved dressing up and looking pretty. She enjoyed hearing people say how pretty and dainty she was. Marian felt a bit scared of the 'exciting games'. She was afraid that Dopey would get excited, too, and gallop about in his mad, clumsy fashion.

Mrs Carlton didn't much like the 'old clothes' idea either. 'Oh, dear. I suppose that means you will play dirty, rough games.'

'And we're having a picnic tea under that big weeping willow,' said John happily.

'How do you know there's a big weeping willow?' asked Annette, at once. 'You've never been into the Taggertys' garden.'

'Shut up,' said John, in a voice exactly like Pat's. His mother stared at him in horror.

'*John!* How *can* you talk like that to Annette? Why, you sounded just like Pat, with his rough talk to poor little Biddy.'

John went red. He really felt a little shocked at himself too. Still, Annette was so awful, the way she kept trying to find out things, and the way she told tales. He didn't say he was sorry, and Mrs Carlton looked quite upset.

'That's what I was afraid of,' she said. 'I thought you would pick up all sorts of horrid ways from those Taggerty children. If only your father hadn't found out that Mr Taggerty was his old school friend!'

'Dopey will be there to play games with us,

too,' said John, trying to change the subject. And, as if he had just heard his name, Dopey appeared, wagging his tail hard, looking at them sideways, as if not quite sure whether he was welcome or not. He had leaped over the wall and come to see them.

'There!' said Mrs Carlton, annoyed. 'I knew that tiresome dog would keep coming here if once we allowed him in. Go away! Shoo, Dopey! Go home, HOME!'

Dopey rolled over on his back and did his bicycling act. He didn't seem to know what the word 'home' meant at all.

'Oh, Mum! He's really very clever, the way he does that,' said John. 'Dopey, we're coming to tea this afternoon.'

'Woof,' said Dopey, rolling himself over on to his four legs and springing upright. He butted John with his head. John was delighted. He patted Dopey, and tickled him behind the ears.

'John, take that dreadful dog back to the Taggertys,' said Mrs Carlton. 'He ran all over the beds, look.'

'Oh, Mum! Let him stay a few minutes,' begged John. 'Anyway, if I do take him back he'll only jump over the wall again.'

'I believe you really do like that nasty dog,' said Marian.

'I do like him and he isn't nasty,' said John.

'You and Annette are such babies. You never like *any* dog.'

'Well, you never did till now,' said Marian, crossly.

'Now don't quarrel,' said Mrs Carlton. 'Oh dear. I do hope you won't end up being like the Taggertys.'

Dopey did not stay very long. He went back to his beloved Taggerty children in a few minutes. But at intervals during the day he leaped over the wall to visit John. John really felt very flattered. Annette would not go down to the bottom of the garden at all, because she was afraid of being leaped on by Dopey, who sprang over the wall very suddenly indeed.

'Like a kangaroo,' said John. 'Honestly, he's a clever dog. He oughtn't to be called Dopey.'

At half past two they put on what their mother called 'old clothes'. Actually they were very nice ones, perfectly clean and tidy. John groaned.

'Couldn't I put on those shorts I've grown out of and that faded jersey, Mum? And look at Annette! That may be her last year's dress, but it looks as good as new. She will never be able to play games.'

'I don't want to,' said Annette, primly.

'Oh, you're hopeless,' said John, putting on Pat's voice again. Annette looked as if she was going to cry. John was about to yell out 'cry-

80

baby' when he saw his mother's face. She looked
annoyed and cross – not a bit like Mum, really.
John felt sure she was about to say that he was
getting just like those Taggertys, so he didn't
yell out 'cry-baby'. He just gave Annette a scornful look and turned away.

They left at ten to three to walk round to the
Taggertys' house. Mrs Carlton wouldn't hear of
them climbing over the wall. She said that wasn't
a proper way of going out to tea at all.

'Now remember your manners,' she said.
'Don't snatch and grab and gobble at teatime
just because the Taggertys do. And remember
to thank Mrs Taggerty for having you. I should
be most ashamed if I had to send you back to
say it, like the Taggertys last night. And come
home at six, please.'

They set off. There were no Taggertys to greet them at the front gate. So they walked primly up the path and knocked at the door. It was opened by a surprised Bridget.

'Well, now, to think you've come all the way round like this! The children are at the bottom of the garden, waiting for you to climb over the wall.'

She took them through the house. It was very untidy. Coats, books, papers, toys, lay about everywhere. Out into the garden they went, and down to the bottom. No Taggertys were to be seen.

'Funny!' said John, staring round. Then suddenly there was a terrifying chorus of screams and yells and whoops, and from under some bushes scrambled the three Taggertys, waving what looked like knives in the air. They fell upon the startled guests, and Annette gave a terrified scream as one of the knives came down on her chest.

'They're killing me! Save me, John!'

But the knives were only made of rubber that bent as soon as the blunt points touched anything. The Taggertys shrieked with laughter at their guests' frightened faces, and threw themselves on the ground to roll about in joy. Dopey rolled with them.

'You frightened me! You shouldn't do that!'

cried Marian, her heart beating fast. Annette was crying, but not very loudly in case Pat should turn on her.

John was sorry for Annette. He put his arm round her. 'Don't cry, silly,' he said. 'It was just their fun.'

'We waited for you to come over the wall, and hid to jump out at you,' said Pat, sitting up. 'Why *didn't* you come over the wall? And I say! Why have you got on nice clothes? We told you not to.'

'These are our old clothes,' said John.

'Well, they look better than our newest ones,' said Maureen. 'I say, didn't we give you an awful fright?'

'Let's have a look at your knife,' said John. He took one. It really did look exactly like a real one. 'I wish I had one like this,' he said. 'It's marvellous!' He drove it into his knee, and the rubber point bent to one side at once. 'Mum would have a fit if she saw this. She'd think it was real.'

'My uncle sent us them,' said Pat. 'If you like I'll write and tell him I've lost mine, then he'll send me another, and I'll give it to you.'

'But you couldn't write a lie like that!' cried Marian. 'You're awful, Pat. You don't seem to think anything of lying and being deceitful.'

'I'll tell Mummy,' said Annette, pursing up

her mouth. At once Biddy flew at her and battered her with her small fists.

'You dare tell on my Pat! You're a tell-tale! I hate you! You dare tell on my Pat!'

Annette was taken aback and almost fell over. Then she lashed out with her fist too and caught Biddy an unexpected blow on her shoulder. Pat roared with laughter.

'Look at the two of them! Go it, youngsters. That's right, hit out, Biddy! Go it, Annette!'

John separated the two angry little girls. 'Stop it,' he said, 'Annette, you're a guest. You can't behave like this.'

'Well, she shouldn't either then!' panted Annette. 'Oh, oh, make Dopey go away!'

Dopey had come up to join in the battle, and was now dancing round on his hind legs, looking alarmingly tall. 'Get down, Dopey,' said Pat. 'Enough, you two kids.'

Annette tried to slap Biddy again. She got a hard push from Pat at once. 'Didn't you hear what I said?' he roared. 'I said "Enough"! And enough it is. You'll do what I tell you when you're here, see?' Annette looked at him, shocked at being pushed like that. John expected her to howl, and to run home to her mother to complain. But she didn't. She went very red and turned away. She turned her back on them all and said nothing.

'Let her alone,' said Maureen. 'She's been so spoilt she doesn't really know how to behave.'

'What shall we play?' said Pat, in an amiable voice. He seemed to forget his spurts of temper immediately. He grinned at John. 'Like to play Indians and see old Dopey wriggling along?'

'Oh yes!' said John at once. 'But I do wish we had really old clothes on. I don't know how we can wriggle in these without making them filthy.'

'Well, your mother won't mind, surely, seeing that we did warn you we wanted to play exciting games,' said Pat. 'Now then – we'll divide into two parties. You can be Big Chief Noise, John, and I'll be Big Chief Feather. Maureen, go and get all the Indian things you can find. Buck up.'

Maureen sped off. 'Oh, are we going to wear Indian things?' asked John, happily.

'You bet,' said Pat. 'And we've got a wigwam too, only we've lost it in the move. It'll turn up sometime, and we can use that for our tent. Now, I'll have Annette for one of my tribe. Come here, Annette. She fights so well she'll be useful to me.'

Annette was startled to hear this. She half turned round, looking in astonishment at Pat. He held out his hand to her. 'Come on, kid. You can be on my side.'

To John's immense surprise, Annette walked

over to Pat, looking pleased. And indeed she felt very pleased. Pat seemed a very strong, rough, fierce kind of boy to Annette, and to be chosen by him like this, after he had given her that hard push, was surprising but somehow very pleasing.

'Then I'll have Biddy,' said John. 'And Marian too. You have Maureen. What do we do? Go stalking one another? Who will have Dopey? Can we?'

'Nobody has Dopey,' said Pat. 'He'll just belong to whatever party he likes. He'll go mad in a minute, when we begin, and wriggle and leap about and do some war-whoops on his own. Here comes Maureen!'

Up came Maureen with her arms full of Indian things. There were six feather headdresses, two of them with trails of feathers that fell from the head to the ground. 'Chiefs' feathers,' said Pat, handing one to John. 'And here's one for you, Annette.'

Annette put it on. She loved dressing up. 'Do I look nice in it?' she asked.

'No, awful,' said Pat at once. He always squashed any attempt at 'showing off' as he called it. 'A perfect fright. Better not wear it.'

But Annette wanted to wear it. She scampered about, feeling thrilled. Dopey capered with her, but for once she didn't mind.

Everyone was soon dressed up. 'It's a pity

Dopey can't wear feathers, too,' said Biddy, eyeing him. 'He'd be a very good Indian dog.'

'No, he wouldn't. He's too noisy,' said Pat. 'Now you go down to the cave-tree, John, with your tribe, and I'll go right to the wall. Then we have to stalk one another and pounce. Prisoners can be taken and tied up – and we'll scalp them!'

Off they all went. Marian was trembling. This game was too exciting, she thought. Oh dear, there was Dopey coming with them. What a very licky dog he was!

9

Marian wants to go Home

The game was indeed exciting. There was a lot of stalking and wriggling over the grass and under bushes, and at the end of it not one single child had tidy or clean clothes. It didn't matter a scrap to the Taggertys, for they all had on the oldest things imaginable, which had been half-dirty anyhow.

But the clean Carlton children soon looked very bedraggled. Annette didn't like it, but she didn't dare to say a word because she was with Pat. As for Marian, she was quite horrified. Only John didn't mind. He was being a real Indian and thinking of nothing else at all.

There was a great deal of yelling and whooping, dancing round, struggling, brandishing of rubber knives, and rolling over and over, with Dopey in the middle of everything. He did some marvellous wriggling on his tummy, but as he was too excited he barked all the time, and wasn't really a good Indian at all.

In the end, John, Biddy and Marian were all captured. Marian and Biddy were condemned by Pat to be tied to trees. John had to lie on the ground and pretend to be dead. But this was very difficult because Dopey didn't seem to understand that he was meant to be dead, and kept pawing at him and giving him great slobbering licks all over his face.

Biddy was used to being tied up to trees. She bore it bravely. But Marian was frightened. Pat had smeared some dirt over his face, and looked most alarming. He yelled in her ear, and brandished his rubber knife over her when he had tied her up.

'You're my prisoner! I shall scalp you!'

'Grrrrr!' growled Dopey, entering into the spirit of the game, and leaping up at poor Marian. She screamed. 'Don't! Don't! I don't like this game. I want to go home. Untie me, untie me!'

Pat thought she was acting. He became even fiercer. Marian screamed piercingly, and John sat up.

'Pat! Shut up! She's really frightened.'

'Good!' said Pat. 'She ought to be frightened. She's my prisoner.'

Someone appeared through the trees. It was Mrs Taggerty. She, too, had heard Marian's piercing screams, and had heard the real fright in them.

'Pat! The child is really frightened,' she said. 'Untie her. I told you not to play rough games with the little Carltons. They're not mad like you are.'

'I want to go home!' wept Marian. 'I hate this game. I hate Pat, I hate Dopey. I want to go home.'

Mrs Taggerty untied her. 'Now, you come and see my baby,' she said.

'I want to go home,' wept Marian, trembling.

Mrs Taggerty put her arm round her. 'Now don't you mind that rough boy of mine,' she said. 'I'll give him a talking to tonight for scaring you so. You shall go home if you want to. But come and see our baby first.'

The others watched her go off with Mrs Taggerty. 'She's a cry-baby,' said Annette, pleased to see Marian crying when she herself wasn't.

'She's not,' said John, loyally. 'You'd have howled your head off too if you'd been tied up and had Pat yelling round you. It's just that she's not used to it.'

'She's a coward,' said Pat.

'I tell you she's not,' said John. 'She's just too gentle for this kind of game. I ought to have thought of it.'

Pat stared at him scornfully. 'Is that how you treat your sisters?' he said. 'Making them namby-pamby little sissies? Pooh!'

'She's scared of lots of things,' said John. 'Dogs and mice and bats and storms – really she is.'

'Well, I hope she never comes here again,' said Pat. 'I don't expect she'll want to, anyhow. What shall we play at now?'

'Let's paddle in the goldfish pond,' said Biddy. 'It's so hot. It would be lovely to get our feet cool and wet.'

'Oooh!' said Annette, surprised. 'Are you allowed to do that?'

'Of course!' Biddy said scornfully, and began to take off her shoes. Maureen and Pat did the same. John and Annette hardly knew what to do. Paddling in the pond! What would their mother say? But it looked so tempting. John peeled off his socks and shoes, too, and so did Annette.

'Mind the goldfish don't nibble your toes, Annette,' said Pat, paddling in the pond. Annette hesitated. She didn't want her toes nibbled.

'Go on! He's only teasing,' said Maureen, giving the little girl a friendly push. 'Haven't you ever been teased before, silly? You'll have to get used to it if you play with us.'

Soon the five of them were happily paddling in the cool water. Then they sat on the edge with their feet still in. 'I wonder what's happened to Marian,' said John. 'I do hope she hasn't gone home. Mum won't like it.'

'What a lot of things your mother doesn't like,' said Pat, wriggling his toes in the water. 'Stop splashing, Dopey. Golly, look at the waves he's making. Your mother must be rather tiresome sometimes, John.'

'Don't say things like that about my mother,' said John, frowning. 'You oughtn't to say things against your parents to anybody. It's a rotten thing to do.'

'All right, all right,' said Pat. 'Look, there's Marian with Mum. She hasn't gone home after all.'

Marian had really meant to go home at once, without any delay at all. But Mrs Taggerty took her to the pram where the baby lay, and showed him to her.

The baby, Michael, lay on his back in the pram with his brilliant blue eyes wide open. He had dark curls clustering all round his head. His lips were very red, and he was as brown as an acorn.

He looked up at Marian, puzzled. Hers was not a face he knew. Marian stared down at him solemnly, tears still wet on her cheeks.

The baby suddenly smiled at her, and chuckled. Then he reached out a small, plump hand, with wrinkles of fat round the wrist, and tried to touch her. She gave him one of her fingers to hold and at once his own baby fingers closed tightly round it. He gurgled.

'Oh!' said Marian in delight. 'He's holding my finger as if he'd never let it go, Mrs Taggerty. And look at him smiling at me! He's lovely – like a real live doll.'

'He is a lovely baby, isn't he?' said Mrs Taggerty. 'They all were, the little rascals, every one of them. Ah, it's nice to see him lying so quiet and good in his pram there, but soon he'll be yelling and rushing round with the rest of them. He likes you, Marian. Hear him gurgling to you!'

'Coo,' said the baby, 'coo-coo. Gah!'

He suddenly tried to sit up, for he was a strong little thing. He still held Marian's finger.

'Do you think I could hold him for a minute?' asked Marian eagerly. 'I've always wanted to hold a real live, warm baby, Mrs Taggerty, but I never have.'

'Of course you can,' said Mrs Taggerty. 'It's nice to see you wanting to fuss him a bit. The others haven't much use for him yet, because he can't play, and he yells if they frighten him. They're a rough lot, the three of them! Now – hold out your arms – that's right! Here he is!'

The sweet-smelling, plump little baby was placed in Marian's outstretched arms. She sighed in delight. He felt so warm and cuddly – better

than any doll she had ever felt. 'He's so sweet,' she said. 'I love him. Can I sit down somewhere and hold him?'

'Well, would you like to sit down on a rug in the sunshine, and cuddle him a bit?' asked Mrs Taggerty, putting a rug down on the grass. 'But don't you want to go home? You go if you want to, dear. I won't keep you here a minute if you don't want to stay.'

'Well,' said Marian, looking down at the smiling baby, 'well – I think I'll stay a bit longer, if you'll let me hold Michael. I do love him.'

She sat there in the sun, nursing the plump baby blissfully. She saw the others paddling, but she took no notice. She was much happier with this gurgling baby!

'I suppose I couldn't sometimes take him out in the pram for you, could I?' she said to Mrs Taggerty, who sat beside her, knitting a blue coat for the baby.

'Well, that would be really sweet of you,' said Mrs Taggerty, gratefully. 'You see, I'm always so busy, and so is Bridget, and none of the children will bother with Michael. They make such a noise in the garden, too, when he ought to be asleep. It would be lovely if you could sometimes wheel him down the road and back.'

Marian felt very happy. She liked all little helpless things like babies and kittens, although she was so scared of even smaller things such as bats and mice. 'I'll come every day of the holidays and take him out,' she promised.

Bridget suddenly appeared with an enormous loaded tray. There were glasses on it, and a large jug of iced lemonade, with the lemon rings still floating in it. There were plates of thick bread-and-butter, and a great jar of golden honey. There were buns cut in half and spread with butter and jam, and an enormous homemade cake.

'Tea!' yelled Pat. 'Hurrah! I thought you'd forgotten us, Bridget! We're going to have it under the willow tree.'

John ran to help Bridget, though Pat made no move to go to her aid at all. Bridget beamed down at John. 'Well, if it isn't nice to see some good manners in a boy! See, Mrs Taggerty, here's a boy who'll help my poor tired old arms. There's manners for you!'

Soon they were all sitting down in the cave-tree, its green light shining over everything. 'Now for a good tuck-in!' said Pat. 'Gosh I'm hungry!'

10

After Tea

Mrs Taggerty took the baby from Marian. 'Do you want to run home to tea now?' she asked. 'I must take the baby in and change him. You run home if you like. And I'll see that rough Pat of mine gets a scolding tonight for scaring you so. He's no right to treat visitors like that and well he knows it.'

'Please don't get him into trouble,' said Marian. 'I don't want that. I feel better now and I don't want to go home. I'd like to go and have tea with the others. It did look so nice.'

'All right,' said Mrs Taggerty. 'I'm glad you don't bear malice. Pat's got a good heart, really, but he's headstrong and he's got no manners at all. I'm hoping maybe you three will teach him some!'

Marian got up and walked over to the others. She went inside the cave-tree. 'Hello! Aren't you going home after all?' asked Maureen.

'No,' said Marian. 'And, Pat, you're not going to be scolded tonight. I asked your mother not to let you be. I don't know why I was so silly and scared.'

Pat grinned his wide grin at Marian. 'Thanks!' he said. 'Sorry I scared you. Only my fun, really. Have a bit of bread-and-butter?'

All six children were very hungry, for the Taggertys had their tea late. They worked their way through the thick, buttery slices of bread, and John discovered that he much preferred a good thick slice to the thin ones he had at home. You could really get your teeth into a thick slice.

The Taggertys had no manners at teatime. Except for the one time that Pat offered Marian the bread-and-butter, nobody passed the Carltons anything. At first they sat patiently with empty plates, waiting to be asked. Then Annette got cross when she saw Biddy spreading honey on her fifth slice of bread-and-butter, without even asking her if she, too, would like some.

'You're awfully rude,' she said to Biddy. 'I've sat here ages with an empty plate. Why don't you offer me something? Don't you know you ought to look after your guests?'

'Can't you help yourself, silly?' said Biddy. 'Grab, like we do, or you won't get anything.'

Mrs Taggerty's voice came across the garden. 'Are you children all right? Pat, are you remembering to look after your guests? Pass them food when their plates are empty and see that they have plenty to eat.'

'Yes, Mum. We're looking after them well!'

Pat called back to his mother at once.

'You are an awful liar,' said John, helping himself to a jammy bun. 'Why can't you say you're not doing your best to look after us, but you will? Anyway, don't bother. I'll help myself. You gobble so fast that if we wait till we're asked we'll get no tea at all.'

Everyone laughed. Maureen actually offered Marian a bun. The buns were lovely. So was the fruity home-made cake. Pat cut the slices, and they were enormous ones. Marian couldn't help comparing them to the thin little slices they had at home. These big, thick slices looked rude and greedy, but they really were lovely and big when you were hungry.

The lemonade was delicious too. The Carltons always had milk for tea at home, and it was

a change to have this lovely sweet lemonade. They enjoyed themselves thoroughly. As for Dopey, he did very well indeed, accepting titbits from all the Taggertys in turn. Socks the black cat joined them too, and ate bits of bread-and-butter very daintily and primly.

'She's funny,' said Pat. 'Although she knows that if she doesn't eat quickly Dopey will gobble up her food, she never will hurry. She reminds me of Marian! You nibble, too, Marian.'

'Does Socks scratch?' asked Marian, rather afraid of the big, green-eyed cat, who suddenly stretched out her front paws and showed her claws.

'Rather!' said Pat. 'Look out she doesn't give you a scratch all down your bare leg.'

'He's only teasing,' said Maureen, seeing Marian's look of alarm. 'It's all right. Socks only scratches if you chase her or pull her tail. Would you like to see my pet mice? I've got three, Woffles, Wiffles and Wonky.'

'Oh *no*!' cried Marian in horror.

'Let's put one down her neck,' suggested Biddy. Marian squealed.

'Be quiet, Biddy,' said John. 'You can see she's afraid.'

After tea Pat suggested a spot of tree-climbing. 'There's a fine chestnut at one side of the garden,' he said. 'Not far from the bottom.

Let's go and climb it. Come on, girls. We'll pretend the tree is a pirate ship – our ship – and that we're sailing to lands far away.'

'What about all these tea things?' asked John. 'Oughtn't we to take them in?'

'Oh, let Bridget,' said Pat, impatiently, and tore off down the garden. Bridget appeared at that moment, and John and Marian helped her to pick up the picnic things and load her tray with them. Annette had disappeared with the others.

'There now! Didn't I say those children had the best manners in the world,' called Bridget to Mrs Taggerty, who was rocking the baby gently in his pram. 'Picked up all the tea things for me, they have, and put them on my tray.'

John and Marian went to join the others. Marian pulled at John's sleeve. 'Don't climb trees! I know I can't. And Mummy wouldn't like it.'

'But we've got old clothes on,' said John, suddenly feeling that he couldn't possibly say he wouldn't climb a tree, and face Pat's scorn. 'You don't need to climb one. But *I* shall.'

'You've never climbed one in your life,' said Marian. 'Never. You'll fall. You just see if you don't.'

Pat was halfway up the tree when they got there. He called down to them, 'Come on. It's great up here. There's a bit of a wind and the tree sways just like a ship at sea.'

Maureen was nearly up to him. Biddy was swarming up too, calling to Maureen to help her.

'Hey, John! Come on up quickly,' shouted Pat. 'We two will watch out for sails on the horizon. Hurry up!'

John valiantly began to climb. He wasn't used to it, and he was, besides, a little afraid of falling. He half-wished he hadn't begun, especially when his shirt caught on a twig and held fast there. He dragged himself away and the shirt tore.

'John's not very good at climbing!' cried Maureen, peering down. 'Do come on, John. Where's Marian? I suppose Annette's too small to come.'

'She's a baby,' announced Biddy, from half-way up the tree. 'She can't climb, can she, Pat? I'm a good climber. You always say so.'

To Marian's immense astonishment, Annette suddenly tried to swing herself up on the first branch. 'I'm coming too!' she shouted. 'I *can* climb. I'm a very good climber! It's Marian that can't climb.'

Annette managed to get quite a long way up the tree. She felt very proud when Pat called down to her, 'Jolly good, Annette. I didn't think you had it in you. Come up higher. John's here.'

But Annette didn't want to go any higher. She was beginning to be afraid. She didn't say so, though. She sat just below Biddy, and peered out between the branches, holding on firmly with both hands.

It was exciting up the tree. John thought it was grand. He felt the tree sway in the wind. He looked down on his own garden, and it seemed very far below. He was excited and pleased. Why had he never climbed a tree before?

All the children forgot the time. Six o'clock had long gone. Now it was quarter to seven. Mr Carlton was home. He and Mrs Carlton walked down to the bottom of the garden to see if there was any sign of the children.

'I told them six o'clock,' said Mrs Carlton, vexed. 'I wonder what they're doing. They made a frightful noise this afternoon. How that Taggerty baby ever manages to go to sleep I don't know.'

They came to the bottom of the garden. They were tall enough to look over the wall, but there were no children to be seen.

Not far off, high above them, were the five children in the tree. Marian was at the foot alone. Pat suddenly saw Mr and Mrs Carlton and gave a loud and piercing yell.

'Hey! Uncle Peter! Mrs Carlton! Here we are!

Up in the tree! Annette is here too. HEY!'

What a shock for the Carlton children's mother! She stared in horror. 'Come down at once!' she said. 'Come down at once!'

The five children gazed down at her. 'Hello, Dad!' cried John. 'Look how high I am!'

Mr Carlton laughed to see so many faces peering out at him from the tree. 'Good for you, John,' he said. 'And is that really Annette I see up there too? Where's Marian?'

'She's afraid to come,' said Annette, importantly. 'But I wasn't. Marian wanted to go home before tea, Daddy.'

'Shut up!' said Pat, John and Maureen all together. Annette shut up. Pat tried to reach her with his foot. 'Tell-tale!' he said.

Mrs Carlton was still looking up in horror. 'John! You know I don't like you to climb trees – and I can't *believe* Annette is up there too! She might fall and break her leg. Peter, go over and get her down before she falls.'

Mr Taggerty came down the garden at that moment and the children waved eagerly.

'Daddy! We're up the chestnut tree! And look, there's Uncle Peter over the wall.'

John saw his mother's displeased, anxious face and began to climb down. Mr Taggerty lifted Annette down. 'There you are! My word, you're just as much of a monkey as Biddy, climbing trees like that!'

Mrs Carlton gazed in dismay at her three children. They were so dirty, so untidy, their clothes were so torn – and surely they were wet, too? What *could* they have been doing with those dreadful Taggerty children?

Mr Carlton lifted them over the wall. Mrs Carlton eyed them in silence. They looked down at their dirty, torn clothes and felt very guilty.

'Well, Mum, we did ask you to let us have old

106

clothes on,' began John. 'It's no good playing in the garden with the Taggertys unless we do.'

'Come along to the house,' said Mrs Carlton, in a cold voice. 'You're very late. I said six o'clock and it's nearly seven.'

They followed her, feeling rather flat after their exciting afternoon. 'Mummy, I nursed the baby,' said Marian. 'He's so lovely and soft.'

Mrs Carlton said nothing. Then Mr Carlton spoke to John. 'I suppose you thanked Mrs Taggerty for having you?' he asked. The three children stopped dead.

'Gracious, no! But it isn't our fault, Daddy. Mummy made us come back so quickly we didn't have time.'

'Well, go back and thank her at once,' said Mr Carlton. 'I'm surprised Mummy didn't say something about it.'

The children went back to thank Mrs Taggerty. Their mother turned to their father. 'I was too upset to think of anything but John and Annette up that high tree,' she said. 'And oh, what little ragamuffins they look. Just like the Taggertys.'

'Never mind. John looked really adventurous for once – and Annette forgot to be a spoilt baby,' said Mr Carlton. 'I only wish Marian had been at the top of the tree too!'

11

A Horrid Quarrel

That was the beginning of the friendship between the Taggerty children and the Carltons. Although Mrs Carlton was cross and disgusted at their appearance when they got back from tea that first time, she did allow them to put on really old clothes the next time. And the Taggertys too appeared in their oldest clothes when they came to play with the Carltons.

John soon began to revel in all the exciting games the Taggertys played, Cowboys and Indians, Burglars and Policemen, Pirates, Dragons, Witches and the rest of them. He became what Mr Carlton called a 'real boy', and actually asked to go with him one afternoon when his father was setting off for one of his long walks.

Annette, instead of hating Pat for his straight speaking, and the way he pushed her when she annoyed him, admired him immensely. She stopped telling tales. She stopped crying. She even stopped showing off, and that was very difficult for her. If only she could be with him she would stand anything, it seemed!

Marian was the only one who didn't like joining in their rough games. 'Well, don't come with us then,' John would say, impatiently. 'Stay at home with your dolls!' But there was one thing that drew Marian to the Taggertys more than any other, and that was the baby. She adored him. All the Taggertys loved him, but only Marian would trouble to cuddle him, and talk to him for hours, and play with him. He loved her.

The Taggertys never seemed to go to church or to Sunday School. They wore the same old clothes on Sunday as on any other day, and they made just as much noise.

'Why do you go to Sunday School this lovely sunny afternoon?' said Pat impatiently one Sunday, when he wanted John to come paddling in the pond with him. 'It's so hot. A paddle would be lovely. And after tea we're going to play shops in the summerhouse. We've got real money. We hoped you'd come.'

'We always do go to Sunday School,' said John. 'And we like it. Why don't you come too? Doesn't your mother want you to go?'

'Yes. But she says it's too much bother to make us,' said Maureen.

'Don't you say your prayers at night either?' asked Annette, who always prayed most fervently, and never forgot to ask God to bless even her smallest doll.

'Sometimes I do,' said Maureen. 'Mostly I forget. It doesn't matter.'

'It *does* matter,' said Marian, shocked. 'If you went to church, and listened to stories at Sunday School, you'd know lots of things you don't seem to know – like why it's wrong to tell as many lies as you do, and why you should be kind to others, and why . . .'

'I don't want to know things like that,' said Pat. 'They're boring. You're goody-goodies! Fancy wanting to go to Sunday School when you could go paddling in our pond. And I thought if Mum wasn't about we might even bathe! Come on, do. You could pretend to start out for Sunday School, but really you could come round to us. You could always say you'd been to Sunday School, if your mother asked you.'

All three Carltons were shocked at this. 'You're hopeless,' said John at last. 'Sometimes I think you're really bad. You'll get an awful punishment some day, I should think. You can tell untruths all you like and be as deceitful as you want to be – but we shan't! We'd like to paddle, and we'd love to bathe – but not if we have to tell stories about it, and deceive Mum! That's not being goody-goody. It's just being deceitful.'

'You don't love your mother if you want to deceive her like that,' said Marian to Pat.

'I do,' said Pat, looking fierce. 'She's the best mother in the world. And yours is awful!'

This was really the last straw. John went flaming red and slapped Pat across the face. 'I'll never speak to you again!' he said.

'Want a fight, do you?' said Pat, his face showing a red mark where John's hand had slapped him. 'All right, come along. I'm ready!'

'Not on Sunday, John! Oh, John, don't fight now. It's time we went to Sunday School,' said Marian, almost in tears. Annette watched in silence, half scared.

'All right,' said John. He turned to Pat. 'I'll fight you tomorrow. Not today. And if you ever dare to say again that my mother's awful, I'll hit you even harder.'

'You're afraid to fight,' said Pat scornfully. 'Cowardy-custard! Afraid to fight! Wants to go to Sunday School instead. Pooh, baby! Go along, then. We won't fight today or tomorrow either. We Taggertys don't want to have any more to do with you at all. Goodbye for ever.'

Pat disappeared. The three Carltons heard footsteps running up the garden. They were all very distressed. 'I shouldn't have hit him like that,' said John. 'But I can't bear him to talk about Mum like that.'

'He's bad, but I do want to play with him again,' whimpered Annette. Marian was white. She took Annette's hand.

'Come along. It's time we went,' she said. 'Oh John – do you think Pat meant what he said? If we never go there again, I'll never see Michael.'

'What's that matter?' said John. 'You're silly over that baby. And I tell you this – and you too, Annette – we are *not* going to have any more to do with the Taggertys.'

And off they went to Sunday School, where poor Marian prayed a very muddled and anxious prayer all about not wanting to play with the Taggertys any more, but please, please, God, could she still see the baby?

They heard the Taggertys screaming and yelling very loudly indeed that evening. 'They can't be playing shops,' said Marian. 'Even they couldn't make such a noise over just shopping. They're playing some noisy game on purpose for us to hear.'

'Shall we tell Mummy what has happened?' asked Annette, who never could resist passing everything on to her mother, much to the annoyance of the others.

'Certainly not,' said John at once. 'That would be sneaking, Annette. Surely you wouldn't be a sneak, after all that everyone has done to stop you?'

'No, I wouldn't,' said Annette. 'Gosh, what a noise! I'm sure all the neighbours will complain.'

They did, and in a short while there was silence at the Taggertys'. Marian said she thought she heard someone crying.

'Perhaps it was Pat getting into trouble,' said Annette.

'Pooh! You know he wouldn't cry out loud,' said John. 'Even if he cried at all! I've never seen him cry yet.'

'You nearly cried yesterday,' said Annette, 'when you twisted your ankle jumping, I saw tears in your eyes, though you pretended to be laughing.'

'Shut up,' said John, fiercely, in a voice like Pat's. Annette shut up. Then the bell rang for her bedtime and she went off.

There was no sign of the Taggertys the next day. The Carltons played in their own garden and they could hear the Taggertys playing in theirs, though they were not nearly so noisy as usual. John, Marian and Annette were playing hide-and-seek after tea, and it was Marian's turn to look for the others. She stood by the wall, counting a hundred, when she heard a whisper.

She looked up. Maureen was peeping over the wall. 'Marian! Our baby's hurt himself. He fell out of his pram.'

Marian's heart stopped still. She forgot all about the dreadful quarrel. 'Where is he?' she asked.

'In his cot,' said Maureen. 'He keeps crying. Mummy said she did wish you'd been in today, because he's always so good with you.'

'I'm coming over,' said Marian at once.

'But Pat says we're never to have anything to do with you again,' said Maureen, looking woebegone.

'I don't care,' said Marian. 'I'm coming over to see Michael. Poor, poor little Michael. Oh, I do hope he'll soon be all right again. Did he hurt his head when he fell?'

She climbed over quickly. Annette, peering out of her hiding-place, was filled with astonishment to see her go over the wall. She called to John.

'Marian's gone to the Taggertys. I saw her!'

'Then she's a nasty, underhand, double-faced untrustable little beast,' said John, trying to think of all the nasty words he knew. 'I said we wouldn't have any more to do with them. Wait till she comes back!'

He wandered off up to the house by himself, very angry. He decided that he wouldn't speak to Marian for days, once he had told her what he thought of her, the nasty little thing!

Annette was left alone at the bottom of the garden. She went to the garden roller and stood on it, wondering if she could see Marian. But Marian wasn't there.

Biddy was there on her way to the wall. She looked up and saw Annette. Annette was about to bob down with a scowl when Biddy called her in a loud whisper. 'Annette! Quick, Annette! I've got some news.'

'What?' asked Annette curiously.

'We've got four dear little kittens!' said Biddy, proudly. 'One's all black, one's tabby, one's black-and-white, and one's exactly like Socks!'

'Do they belong to Socks?' asked Annette, thrilled.

'Yes, she had them last night,' said Biddy. 'She's licked them till they're lovely. Come and see them.'

'John said —'

'I know. So did Pat,' said Biddy. 'But you simply *must* see the kittens. Socks is so proud of them. She's in a basket in the kitchen. I know we're in the middle of a quarrel but we didn't know Socks was having kittens, and you really must see them while they're so weeny.'

Annette climbed over the wall. Soon she was in the kitchen with Biddy, and the two of them were looking with delight at the four tiny kittens beside Socks. Socks purred proudly and licked each one.

'Oh, how I would like that one that's just like Socks!' said Annette. 'We've never never had a pet, not even a cat to kill the mice. I do wish I could have a kitten.'

'I'll give you the one like Socks, if you like – if Mummy says I can,' said Biddy. 'And I'm sure she will. You can have it for your own when it's old enough. It would be better than any doll.'

'Oh, Biddy! Ask your mother,' begged Annette. 'And I'll ask mine, but mine will be the difficult one. She doesn't like animals.'

'Well, ask your father then,' said Biddy. 'He likes animals, doesn't he? Even our pet mice. He'll make your mother let you have it. You ask him.'

This seemed a very good idea indeed. Annette stroked Socks and began to plan all kinds of things for the kitten – a blue ribbon – a fine basket – a little ball!

John couldn't find Annette when he went down the garden again. He looked at the wall. Surely Annette hadn't gone over too? What were the two girls thinking of? He felt very angry indeed.

I'll go over too! he thought. And I'll find Pat, and make him take back what he called me – a cowardy-custard indeed. If he doesn't – I'll fight him!

12

Making It Up

John climbed over the wall and went into the Taggertys' garden. No Annette, no Biddy, no Maureen, no Marian. Not even Dopey! How strange. Suddenly he heard a dismal whining. It came from the garden shed. It was so very dismal that John couldn't bear it. Dopey was locked up. Why? He crept cautiously to the shed door. He looked in at the window. Pat was sitting with his arm round Dopey's neck. To John's intense surprise Pat was crying. Yes, a tear actually rolled down his cheek. What was up? He opened the door and went in. Pat glared up at him, and wiped away the one tear fiercely.

'Get out!' he said.

'What's up?' asked John.

'Dopey went mad this afternoon when we were playing some jumping game, and he leaped on top of the pram and knocked it half over,' said Pat. 'Baby fell out and hurt himself. And Bridget got a stick and hit Dopey till he cried. He's still crying. I can't bear it. Dopey didn't mean to knock the pram over.'

Dopey whined dolefully. He didn't understand

why he had been hit. He nestled closer to Pat.

John forgot what he had come for. He was very upset about Dopey, too. 'Didn't Bridget understand that he did it by accident?' he said indignantly, and sat down on the other side of the big dog. Dopey gave a long sigh and licked John on the nose. 'How mean of Bridget! How long is Dopey to be locked up?'

'Till he's given away,' Pat said mournfully, and looked so miserable that John couldn't bear it.

'Given away! Do you mean to say Dopey's got to go?' he asked in horror.

'Well, that's what they all say,' said Pat. 'I can't live without him. Nobody believes me when I say that, but it's true.'

John felt quite certain it was true. He was sure he would feel the same if Dopey belonged to him. Dopey was so idiotic and lovable and eager and affectionate. John's heart sank when he thought that Dopey might be sent away and never come back again.

'Pat,' he said in a low voice, 'we'll see that he isn't sent away. I could hide him in our shed, if only he wouldn't make a noise.'

Pat looked hopeful for a moment. Then he shook his head. 'But he *would* make a noise. You know he would. Thanks awfully all the same, John.'

There was a silence. Dopey whined a little and the two boys patted him. 'What did you come for?' asked Pat, after a while. 'Did you want something?'

'Well,' said John, looking uncomfortable, 'I really came over to fight you, as a matter of fact. You made me so angry, you know.'

'You made me angry, too,' said Pat. 'You'd better not slap me again like that.'

'I'm sorry about that,' said John, 'especially now I know about Dopey.'

'We'd better be friends again, hadn't we?' said Pat. 'I take back all I said. I'm sorry.'

John felt better at once. 'So do I,' he said, and for once he bore no malice, but felt exactly the same towards Pat as he had done before the quarrel.

Marian was indoors with the baby. Mrs Taggerty was there, looking worried. But since

Marian had come Michael was happier. He had stopped crying and had taken hold of Marian's finger in the way she loved. Then he suddenly smiled at her.

'Look at that!' said Mrs Taggerty, relieved. 'He'd not smile like that unless he was feeling himself again, bless him. He's getting over the shock. He'll soon be all right.'

'I'd better go back home now,' said Marian, getting up. 'I didn't tell Mummy I was coming, and she may be wanting me. I'm so glad Michael's better, Mrs Taggerty. I'll come in tomorrow to play with him, shall I?'

'Yes, do,' said Mrs Taggerty. 'He's always so good with you. Hello, here's little Annette!'

Annette tiptoed in with Biddy. Marian looked at her in surprise. Why had she climbed over the wall? Had she disobeyed John too?

'Mrs Taggerty,' began Annette, eagerly, in a whisper, 'could I have one of Socks's new kittens, please, when it's old enough – if Mummy says I may? Please do let me. I'll take such care of it. I shall call it Whitefeet.'

'Yes, of course you can,' said Mrs Taggerty, smiling. 'You ask permission and you can certainly have little Whitefeet. What a pretty name!'

Annette's face glowed. She was just about to thank Mrs Taggerty when somebody else tiptoed into the room. This time it was John. He looked most surprised to see Marian and Biddy there, and they both looked guilty.

'Mrs Taggerty,' began John, 'Pat is upset about Dopey being sent away. Couldn't you please keep him? He didn't mean to knock the pram over. I'm sure he'll never do it again. Pat's so miserable.'

Marian and Annette stared at John in surprise. Why, surely John had a fierce quarrel with Pat, and was never, never going to have any more to do with him.

'Will you keep Dopey?' asked John. 'Dopey would pine away if you didn't, Mrs Taggerty. Please keep poor Dopey. Pat would die without him! You wouldn't like that.'

'I would not,' said Mrs Taggerty, and a little tiny twinkle came in her eyes. 'Well, we'll see. Maybe if Pat tries not to be so noisy when Baby is asleep, and keeps Dopey quiet too, I'll keep him.'

'Oh, thank you, Mrs Taggerty!' said John, fervently. 'How's Michael?'

But without waiting for an answer he sped off to find Pat and tell him that Dopey might not be sent away after all. The others followed him. Soon they were all in the garden shed comforting Dopey, who enjoyed the attention very much indeed. Even Marian was glad that he wasn't to be sent away, for she too knew he had upset the pram by accident.

'Well – the quarrel's ended,' said Pat, looking round at everyone with his usual grin. 'Funny! I was absolutely determined never to speak to any of you again – and here we are, the best of friends. You were very decent about it, John.'

After that things went on much the same as usual. Dopey was not sent away. Michael soon recovered from the shock of falling out of his pram, and he really had not hurt himself very much. Annette's kitten grew rapidly, and she watched it squirming about in Socks's basket every day, and wondered when she dared ask her father if she could have it.

She had quite decided not to ask her mother. Mrs Carlton would say no at once. But her father liked animals. She wondered if he would think she had gone behind her mother's back, if she asked him first and said nothing to Mummy about it?

Fortunately her birthday was coming along soon, and people always asked her what she wanted most. Her father would too. Then she could ask about the kitten.

Sure enough, one morning Mr Carlton asked her the question she was waiting for. 'Well, Annette? You'll be five soon. What do you want for your birthday?'

'There's something I want most terribly,' said Annette. Mr Carlton smiled.

'What is it? A new doll?'

'No. Something much, much nicer,' said Annette. 'And oh, Daddy, it won't cost you any money at all. But it's something I'll really love to have for my very own.'

'Whatever is it?' asked Mr Carlton, curiously. Mrs Carlton smiled, too, wondering what made Annette so serious.

'I want a kitten,' said Annette, earnestly. 'The one I want belongs to Socks, and it's exactly like her. Biddy says I can have it, and Mrs Taggerty says so too. Can I, Daddy?'

'I don't see why not,' began her father, and the three children whooped in delight. Annette flung herself on her father. 'Daddy! Thank you!

I'm going to call it Whitefeet and I'm saving up for a basket for it.'

Mrs Carlton didn't say anything. She didn't want a cat in the house, but how could she bear to disappoint her precious little Annette, when Peter had already said he didn't see why she shouldn't have the kitten? Oh dear. Those Taggertys were at the bottom of everything.

Annette flew to tell Biddy. The two little girls told Socks, and she listened, purring. 'I'll be very, very good to your kitten, Socks,' said Annette. 'You can trust me. I'll love it and look after it well. Just as well as you look after them all.'

There were no more big quarrels after that. The two families were beginning to respect one another, and copy one another too. John was much more adventurous, to his father's delight. Marian was no longer scared of Dopey, and even consented to look at the pet mice. Annette was full of respect and admiration for Pat, who ordered her about and ticked her off just as he did Biddy.

Annette no longer told tales, and only cried when the others were not there. She didn't dare to show off any more in front of the Taggertys, and was a nicer little girl altogether.

And the Taggertys even copied the Carltons in a few ways! Their manners were better, they didn't think it was so clever to tell lies, though they still told them. Pat was more gentle to Biddy and Maureen, as John was to his own sisters. The two fathers were pleased to see the effect each family had on the other.

'They're so different,' said Mr Taggerty. 'Yours are so gentle, compared with mine, and I must say they are very well brought up, Peter, and have some very nice ideas. Mine are a set of ragamuffins, I know.'

'Oh, they're a fine set of children,' said Mr Carlton warmly. 'They've done mine a lot of good, as I thought they would. I got worried about John – a little mother's boy he seemed to me – but now that he climbs trees and goes for walks and rags about with the others, he's quite different.'

The two fathers often talked together, renewing their old schoolboy friendship. The two mothers sometimes called on one another and talked too.

Mrs Carlton grew to like the lively, cheerful, easy-going Mrs Taggerty. She saw how much her children loved her and clung round her, though they were sometimes cheeky and disobedient.

And Mrs Taggerty liked and admired the neat, well-dressed Mrs Carlton, and sighed when she thought how beautifully she had brought up her three children, and how badly-behaved the

Taggertys always seemed to be, compared with the Carltons.

'I suppose it's my fault,' she said to Mrs Carlton, over a cup of tea one afternoon. 'If children are left to themselves they just grow into little scamps. I don't believe mine know Sundays from weekdays!'

'Well, that's easily put right,' said Mrs Carlton. 'I'd be very pleased to take them to church with us on Sundays, and they could go to Sunday School in the afternoons with mine, too. They do so love all they do at Sunday School, you know.'

'Oh, mine wouldn't go if I asked them!' said Mrs Taggerty.

Mrs Carlton thought it a great pity. Her own three hadn't had much effect on the Taggertys in some ways. She rose to go. 'Well, goodbye, Mrs Taggerty, I *have* enjoyed coming to tea with you.'

13

I Dare You!

The cave-tree, the pond and the summerhouse were all lovely places to play games in. The cave-tree could be a big wigwam, a cave inside a green mountain, a house and all kinds of things. The pond could be the sea, or a big lake. It was never just a pond. The summerhouse could be a house to live in, a shop, a school, a castle, and half-a-hundred other things.

Compared with their own garden, the garden of the Taggertys seemed a perfect playground to the Carltons. Mrs Carlton could never understand why.

'Our garden is so much nicer,' she said. 'The beds are full of flowers, the paths are trimly kept, the grass is properly cut. Why do you always want to go into the Taggertys' garden?'

'Oh – it's much more exciting!' said John. 'But Mum, we're going to help Mr Taggerty to tidy up the top part, near the house. He's asked us to. I do think Pat and the others might help him, but they won't.'

It was a funny thing, but though Pat would tire himself out playing Indians, or chasing for hours up and down the garden, he was always too tired or too lazy to help to tidy up the garden, to carry things for Bridget, or even to fetch anything for his mother.

He didn't mind taking Dopey for long walks, but he didn't want to run down to post a few letters. He would climb every tree in the garden one after another, but he wouldn't wheel Michael down the road and back.

Still, that didn't matter, because Marian was always on hand for that. She never minded what she did for Michael. Mrs Taggerty often said she wished she were her own little daughter, she was so useful.

'Don't you like Michael?' Marian asked Maureen. 'You never do anything for him.'

'Oh yes, I like him. I love him,' answered Maureen. 'But it's such a bore, always having to be quiet when he's asleep. And I hate having to wheel him out.'

'You don't really love him, if you don't want to do things for him,' said Marian. 'You're rather selfish, I think, Maureen. Still, I don't mind, because it means I can do the things you don't want to do but which *I* love to do!'

Dopey came running up at this moment. He certainly could be a very stupid dog, but stupid or not he seemed to realise that it was very important not to jump about anywhere near the pram now. He stopped short every time he came to it, and put his tail down. He was very interested in Socks's kittens, and bore several scratches on his nose which Socks had given him for his curiosity.

Annette was impatient because her kitten did not grow as quickly as she wanted it to. It took twelve days to get its eyes open. 'Fancy, twelve days!' said Annette. 'I thought it would be blind for ever! It's got dear little blue eyes just like all the Taggerty family have.'

She was looking forward very much to having the kitten for her own. Mrs Carlton had said that it was to be house-trained before they had it, and that if it was dirty she could not keep it. Annette was very anxious for it to behave itself well.

'I do hope it will have nice manners,' she said to Marian. 'But it can't learn very good ways from the Taggertys, really. I like them all, now, but I still think they are very dirty and untidy – and they do say such cheeky things to Bridget.'

'Socks will teach the kitten to wash itself and keep clean and nice,' said Marian. 'Socks always looks very tidy and clean, doesn't she? I wish we could buy a baby, too, Annette. A little tiny one, so that it would take a long time to grow. If Michael gets much heavier I shan't be able to lift him.'

John could never do the daring things that Pat did, because, though he enjoyed climbing and jumping and wading in the river, he was always a little afraid of doing some of Pat's most reckless things.

'You're bigger than I am,' he said to Pat one day. 'And stronger. If I tried to do all the things you do, I'd end up breaking my leg or something. So what's the sense?'

One afternoon Pat dared John to jump over a stream that ran in the meadow not far from their house. John looked at it. It was wide and deep just there, and ran strongly.

'You couldn't jump over it just here yourself,' he said to Pat. 'You do the dare yourself, before you challenge me, see?'

'I can easily do it!' said Pat. He went a little way back, measured the stream with his eye, ran forward swiftly and jumped. He sailed right over the stream and landed well over the other side.

'Well done!' cried John.

'I *could* do it, you see!' shouted Pat, triumphantly. 'Oh, here comes Dopey. He can do it too. Well done, Dopey! You're braver than John. He doesn't dare.'

'It isn't that,' cried John. 'I just know I *can't* do it! I shall only fall in the middle and wet myself to the skin. Then I'll get into a good old row and not be allowed out with you again. It

isn't that I don't dare. I'll jump the stream further down the field, if you like, where it isn't so wide.'

But Pat was obstinate. 'No. Jump it here. You say you won't because you're afraid. We always said you were namby-pamby, but I thought you'd grown out of it – and you haven't. Pooh!'

John flushed red. He looked at the stream. No, it was no good, he couldn't jump it. All right then, let Pat think what he liked. He turned to go home, sulking.

Pat laughed. 'Old gloomy-face! You'll turn the milk sour and the butter rancid if you go home like that.'

'Well, stop saying I don't dare to do this and that, then,' said John furiously. 'You can't tell the difference between being reckless and being sensible, that's what's the matter with you. Why should I get myself soaked just to please you? It's nothing to do with my being brave. I could be brave enough if there was any need for it, you know that. I suppose you think you're brave enough for anything – you wouldn't be afraid of a single thing.'

'No, I wouldn't,' boasted Pat. 'I dare to do anything!'

The boys went home. John was rather quiet. He was trying not to sulk, but it was difficult. Pat was lively and cheerful, in a teasing mood. The boys parted at the Taggertys' gate and John went home.

After tea he and Marian and Annette went down the garden to play. 'Shall we go over the wall?' asked Annette. John shook his head.

'No. Let's play here for a change.'

Over the wall an exciting game was going on. The Taggertys were doing something with a cricket ball. There were shouts and laughter – and then a fearful crash! It came from the garden next to the Taggertys'.

'Whew! Their ball has gone into the Johnsons' cucumber frame,' said John. They listened. There was a dead silence from the Taggertys' garden. Not a word, not a laugh.

'They've fled indoors, I should think,' said

John. 'My word, I bet Miss Johnson will be angry. She's always complaining about the Taggertys.'

Footsteps came down the Johnsons' garden, and there was an angry exclamation. Miss Johnson leaned over the broken glass in the cucumber frame and picked up the cricket ball which lay among her cucumbers.

She caught sight of the three Carlton children and called to them, 'Is this your ball? Did you break my frame?'

'No, Miss Johnson,' said John at once. 'We didn't.'

'Then who did?' cried Miss Johnson. 'There doesn't seem to be anyone in the Taggertys' garden. Did you see the Taggertys throw the ball over into my garden?'

'No, Miss Johnson,' answered John, truthfully. He felt awkward. He couldn't tell tales of the Taggertys. He wished they would come out and own up.

Apparently Pat did come out. He walked whistling down the garden, his hands in his pockets. Miss Johnson called out to him.

'Pat! Is this your ball?'

Pat stopped, and looked surprised. 'Oh no! That's not ours, Miss Johnson. Where did you find it?'

'In my cucumber frame,' said Miss Johnson,

grimly. 'Somebody threw it over the wall and broke the glass. Are you sure it wasn't you?'

'Oh yes, quite sure, Miss Johnson,' said Pat, still looking very innocent. 'I'm so sorry about it. Who could have thrown it?'

Miss Johnson snorted and went back into the house with the cricket ball. Pat looked over the wall and grinned.

'Phew! We only just ran away in time,' he said. John stared straight at him.

'I'm going to dare you to do something,' he said, in a cold, scornful voice. 'You laughed at me because I wouldn't jump the stream, but I knew I couldn't. Now I'm going to dare you to do something you *can* do – but you'll be afraid, and I shall laugh at *you*! We all shall.'

'I'll take the dare,' said Pat at once.

'Very well. Go and own up to Miss Johnson and tell her you broke the frame and told a lie,' said John. 'Go on. I dare you to!'

Pat looked taken aback. 'That's a silly dare,' he began, but John interrupted him.

'It isn't. I'm just showing you what a coward you are. You don't dare to own up when you've done wrong. That's much more cowardly than not daring to jump a stream that's too wide. You're not brave, Pat. You can climb a tree and jump a stream – but you can't own up to anything. Coward! I'm ashamed of having you for a friend.'

John turned and went up the garden with Annette and Marian. Both girls thoroughly agreed with him. They never could understand why Pat should be so cowardly and deceitful over things like this, when he always seemed so brave in other things.

Pat stood for a minute, thinking. At first he

felt angry. Then he flushed. He saw that John was right. He was afraid of owning up. He always had been. And Maureen and Biddy were just the same.

John always owned up at once, no matter how he might be punished. He was brave and good that way. Pat suddenly felt ashamed of himself. He rushed indoors and found his money-box, and took out his birthday five pounds. Then he ran round to Miss Johnson's front door and hammered on it. He must do this thing while he still felt so ashamed. If he waited he might change his mind.

Miss Johnson opened the door in surprise. 'Miss Johnson – I broke your frame. I'm very sorry I said I didn't,' said Pat, his words tumbling out in a hurry. 'I've brought you the money to pay for new glass.'

He thrust the money into the surprised Miss Johnson's hands and ran off again. He had owned up! It was horrid and difficult, but he had done it. He went home again and tore down to the bottom of the garden. He shouted loudly.

'John! Come here! I want you!'

John came, still looking cold and scornful. 'I've taken your dare!' said Pat, grinning suddenly. 'I've owned up and I've told Miss Johnson I told a lie to her. I've given her the money for the frame out of my money-box. Say you're not ashamed to have me for a friend, John. I won't make you ashamed that way again. You're quite right about it.'

'Good for you!' said John, really touched, and he thumped Pat on the back. 'You're really brave. I always knew you were. Good for you! I almost feel I'll go and jump that stream now – and get right over it, too!'

14

Going to School

'Only two more days before we go back to school,' said Pat, gloomily. He was swinging on a low bough of a tree in his garden, and John was sitting beside him.

'Well, I like school,' said John. 'You're coming to my school, aren't you, Pat? It'll be nice to go with you each morning. But you'll have to go clean and tidy, and I'd better warn you that our form master goes up in smoke if we walk about with our hands in our pockets.'

'It sounds as bad as the school I went to before,' groaned Pat. 'I hate school. Always having to do as you're told, and having to sit still, and swot at things you don't like and . . .'

'If you sit next to me I'll help you,' said John. He guessed that Pat was lazy and difficult at school. It was likely that he would be cheeky too – and old Potts, the form master, wouldn't stand that. Pat would find himself robbed of football, and having to stay in and write out *I must be polite* a hundred or more times.

'The only things I shall like about the new school are break and football,' said Pat. 'And I don't think it's worth going to school for those two things. I wish I could run away to sea!'

This was one of Pat's stock wishes when he had to face things he didn't like. John laughed.

'If you went to sea you'd find things a lot harder than being at school, idiot, and you'd get plenty of shouts and roars and clips on the ear. Hello, there's Maureen – and Marian with the baby as usual. She's mad on that baby.'

'Well, let her be,' said Pat, swinging himself so violently that John fell off the branch to the ground. 'Hey, Marian! Can't you leave Michael alone even for a moment?'

'I shall have to in two days' time,' said Marian, gloomily. 'School opens then. Maureen and I are going to the same school, just as you and John are. There will just be Biddy and Annette left to play with each other, and poor Michael will be all alone.'

'He'll have Dopey,' said Pat, and the big dog came running up, hearing his name. 'I wouldn't mind going to school a bit if Dopey could come too. He did keep coming to my last school, till the master complained, and then he had to be tied up all the morning. Shame!'

Dopey floundered round in his usual idiotic fashion. Marian pushed him away from Michael. She really didn't mind Dopey a bit now; she had got used to him and his silly, lovable ways, and except when he barked very suddenly she liked him. As for John, he agreed with Pat that Dopey was the nicest dog in the world.

Annette arrived over the wall, beaming. She no longer looked always as if she was about to go to a party. Mrs Carlton had bought her some shorts, and she wore them in the garden, looking much more sensible in them than in her pretty little dresses.

'Hello!' she said to everyone. 'Mummy's been writing out invitations to my birthday party. She's written one out for you, Pat, and Maureen and Biddy – and for lots of others too.'

Pat and Maureen didn't look very thrilled. They didn't like the kind of parties they had to dress up for. 'When is it?' asked Pat.

'Next Wednesday,' said Annette. 'And your mother says I can have Socks's kitten that day, because it will be old enough to leave its mother. That will be my very nicest birthday present.'

Marian loved a party. 'There'll be ice creams, and lots of sandwiches and crisps and sausage rolls and a big birthday cake with five candles on,' she said. 'It will be a lovely party.'

'I shall like that part of it,' said Pat. 'I suppose we shall go from school, John, shan't we? We won't have time to clean ourselves up much, or put on party things.'

'Wednesday is a half-holiday,' said John.

'We'll have plenty of time to get ready.'

'I wish Michael could come,' said Marian.

'Goo,' said Michael, staring up at the moving green leaves above his head.

'Well, he can't,' said Pat. 'You'll be mooning over him the whole time if he does, and won't join in any games at all. You spoil him. I'll have an awful time licking him into shape when he can walk and talk.'

'You jolly well won't lick him into shape,' said Marian fiercely, hugging Michael close.

'Well, I shall,' said Pat. 'I'd be a poor elder brother if I didn't. I shan't let him be a mollycoddle like John used to be.'

'A Marian-coddle you mean,' said John, with a giggle at his own wit. 'What shall we play? We'd better make the most of what time we've got left – school will soon begin.'

Then they plunged into a terrifically noisy game of Pirates, in which Annette joined with gusto, and Dopey enjoyed tremendously. He waited till first one child rolled on the ground and then another, then leaped on the heap, licking so ferociously that it was almost unbearable.

'We ought to keep a towel handy when Dopey joins in our games,' said John, wiping his face with his handkerchief. 'He really has got the wettest tongue in the world. Stop it, Dopey. If you lick me again I'll lock you up.'

'Woof,' said Dopey, which meant 'Liar!' He knew that not one of the children would ever lock him up or tie him. It was only the grown-ups who did that.

School came two days later. Pat and John set off together. Pat looked unusually clean for him, and actually wore new trousers. His wavy hair was as smooth as he could get it. John stared at him.

'You don't look like yourself a bit. Did your mother make you look so neat?'

'Yes. She's taking a leaf out of your mother's book, and nags at us about clean hands and cleaning our teeth and keeping our clothes decent now,' said Pat, in disgust. 'She never did before.'

Maureen set off with Marian, but to her disappointment she was put into a class below. And Pat, to his dismay, was also placed in a form below John. Now they wouldn't be together.

'Dad won't like hearing we're below you and Marian,' he grumbled at break. 'He's so clever himself, he thinks we must be clever too. And now he'll think we aren't.'

'Well, you can easily go up into my form, if you work hard enough,' said John. 'You're cleverer than I am in some things. Anyway, you'll be miles better at gym and games.'

Pat was. He was soon one of the stars in the football team, sturdy, quick, fearless and a very fast runner. John was quite good, but too afraid of being hurt to be first class. He was not as reckless at Pat either, and his overcautiousness made him miss many good chances of playing really well. Still, he was much better than he had been before, mostly because he was copying Pat and trying to be as plucky as he was.

Maureen grumbled about being below Marian. 'I don't see why I am. I'm sure I could do the same work as you do. Why are you higher than me? You're the youngest in your form, but I shouldn't have thought you were as clever as all that.'

'I'm not,' said Marian, honestly, 'but Mummy always helps me a lot at home, you know, and explains things to me I don't understand, and shows me how to do things. That's really why I've got on, I think.'

'My mother never does that,' said Maureen. 'She just doesn't bother with us like yours does. Sometimes I think it's a good thing not to be fussed over like you are – but other times I wish my mother would help us a bit more. I couldn't possibly go and ask her to help me with those awful homework sums for instance. And Daddy wouldn't bother either. Still, I'd hate to be fussed over always, as you are.'

Marian said nothing. Neither she nor John would discuss their mother with the Taggertys. They loved her very much even though they sometimes wished she wouldn't fuss so. They liked Mrs Taggerty too, and secretly thought that the three Taggerty children were very lazy and selfish and rude towards their mother.

'They don't do a thing for her,' said John once to Marian. 'Anyone would think they didn't love her.'

'Sometimes I wonder if they do,' said Marian. 'How can you be so mean to somebody if you really do love them? Why, yesterday Maureen wouldn't even lay the table for her mother when Bridget was out. She just ran out into the garden. I was there and saw her. I think it's funny really the way Mrs Taggerty treats those three. Sometimes she loses her temper with them, sometimes she just says nothing.'

'I don't think they love Mrs Taggerty,' said John. 'Not really. Or their father either. I like them, they're fun, and it's nice to share Dopey and Socks with them, and play their exciting games – but they hardly ever think of anyone but themselves.'

Pat and Maureen soon settled down at their new schools. Maureen liked it. She hadn't liked her other school, because she hadn't known how to behave, and had been a rough, ill-mannered little girl whom both teachers and children disliked. But now she knew better and she enjoyed being liked.

Pat loved the gym and the football, but he groaned at the work. He messed up his homework and refused John's offer to help him. 'No. If you come over and help me we'll be ages. I don't care if I'm bottom of the form or not so long as I'm in the football team.'

'But your father will be wild when you get a bad report,' said John.

'Well, perhaps if he'd taken the trouble to help me when I first began school, likes yours did, I wouldn't be so bad at lessons,' said Pat. 'Now shut up lecturing, John. Did you see me climb up to the very top of the gym rope today? I bet I looked like a monkey.'

'And that's just what you are,' said Maureen, unexpectedly. 'You're a monkey!'

15

Annette has a Birthday

Annette's party was a great success. Twenty children came, all bringing little presents. Annette was full of pride and delight. She had a new blue dress with a lovely sash, and blue socks and shoes to match. She looked very pretty, and knew it.

'Don't I look nice?' she cried, dancing over to Maureen, who had just arrived with Pat and Biddy. 'Do you like my new dress?'

'It's awful,' said Pat at once and Annette pouted.

'You don't really mean it!' she said.

'Well you're awful, anyway, showing everyone how vain you are,' said Pat. But Annette wouldn't listen. She would have burst into tears two months back, but now she had got used to being teased and was much more sensible. All the same she didn't show off any more, but welcomed her guests politely.

It was a lovely party. There were balloons and crackers and games. There was a glorious tea, but unfortunately Annette was so excited that she could hardly eat anything.

'She's always like that at parties,' said Marian

to Biddy, who was tucking in fast. 'You don't need to gobble so, Biddy. There's plenty of time and plenty of food. You ought to have been a turkey, you're such a gobbler.'

'Well, I'd rather be a gobbler than somebody like Annette who feels sick at parties,' said Biddy. 'What an awful waste!'

The birthday cake candles were lit. They were so pretty, two green, two red and one yellow. Annette cut her cake, with her mother guiding her hand, and soon everyone had a piece of the delicious cake on his or her plate. Pat and Biddy had two pieces each, of course. Maureen would

have liked another, but just couldn't manage it.

'What bad manners those Taggerty children have!' said one of the children's mothers, who had come to help, to Mrs Carlton. 'Look how they grab and gobble.'

'Yes. But they're much better than they used to be,' said Mrs Carlton. 'Really they are. I do think my three have been a good example to them. I'd like them to go to Sunday School with mine, and I've offered to take them to church with us any Sunday morning – but no, Mrs Taggerty just won't tell them to go, because they don't want to.'

'What a pity!' said the other mother. 'Such nice looking children too – and I hear the baby is a beauty. But dear me, how Miss Johnson complains of them. Says they make more noise than any children in the place. I'm glad I don't live next to them.'

Annette was a very good hostess. She really did look after her guests well. Most of them were her own age, and she saw that each of them had a balloon and two crackers. She watched for anyone who was left out of anything, and went to make them join in. Mrs Carlton was very pleased with her.

John was good too. He was always gentle with little children for that had been his father's teaching. Maureen watched him picking up a boy who had fallen, and giving another his balloon when his had burst. Then she turned to find Pat. He was teasing a small girl. He had taken her balloon away and was snatching it out of her reach every time she tried to get it.

She felt a sudden feeling of affection for good-hearted John and of annoyance with Pat. Why must he always tease and be rough and annoying? she thought. Everyone must think he's so badly behaved.

Of the three Taggerty children, Maureen was the one who most liked and admired the Carltons. She especially liked John. He was always kind to her, even in the roughest of games, and never wilfully hurt her as Pat did.

The party came to an end all too quickly. The Taggertys were, as might have been guessed, the very last to go, and they wouldn't have gone when they did if Mrs Carlton hadn't firmly said they must. They remembered to thank her and Annette for the lovely party. Annette gave Biddy a hug.

'Thank you for Whitefeet!' she said warmly. 'He's my nicest present of all. I've had three dolls and a doll's pram and books and games and toys – but I like my sweet little kitten best of all. I do hope he won't miss Socks too much.'

'Oh, Socks is tired of all her kittens now,' said Biddy. 'She smacks them hard when they jump at her tail. She'll be glad that one of them is gone. The others will soon go too. I don't expect Whitefeet will miss Socks at all.'

But little Whitefeet did! He missed his big, warm, comfortable mother and his playful brothers. He mewed pitifully and Annette could hardly bear it. She cuddled him in her arms after she had had her bath that night, and comforted him.

'Don't cry, Whitefeet. I love you. I'll take care of you just as well as Socks did. Don't cry! Mummy, let me take him to bed with me, he's so unhappy.'

Mrs Carlton was shocked. Take a kitten to bed! What next? It was bad enough to have one in the house, without letting Annette take him into her bed.

'Certainly not,' she said.

'Not even on my birthday?' said Annette, pleadingly.

'Not even on your birthday,' said Mrs Carlton firmly, so there was no more to be said.

Annette went to bed and fell asleep thinking of Whitefeet. She woke in the middle of the night and remembered. Was he crying?

Annette had to go and see. She slipped down the dark stairs and went to the kitchen, where Whitefeet had been put into a cosy basket. She opened the door and switched on the light.

Whitefeet was sitting up in his basket, wide awake. His eyes shone brightly. He gave a little welcoming mew and tumbled out of the basket. He was still so small that it was quite difficult for him to reach the ground. He ran to Annette and she picked him up. 'Are you all right?' said the little girl. 'Are you unhappy? You don't miss Socks, do you?'

She sat down in a comfortable wicker chair, with the kitten on her knee. Whitefeet patted a button on her nightie, and then tried to nibble it. Then he settled down in a little round ball, making a warm patch on Annette's knees, and went to sleep.

Annette loved feeling him there. Marian may like to hold Michael and feel how soft and warm he is, she thought, but I think a kitten is much nicer. I don't like to get up. If I do he'll wake and begin to mew. I'll just stay with him for a while.

So she stayed – and, of course, she fell fast asleep too. When morning came, Annette stumbled up to bed, sleepy and stiff. Whitefeet, thoroughly awake, began to play with the rugs and was very happy indeed. Then he began to look for his brothers.

The kitten was a great success. All the children loved it and its funny, playful ways. It would hide under beds and jump out at people's passing legs. It would go to sleep on Mr Carlton's feet, and it would sometimes go completely mad and tear round and round the room without stopping.

Mr Carlton loved it, too. 'I had a kitten as mad as Whitefeet when I was a boy,' he said. 'It was called Bimbo. And I had a puppy too, called Sandy, because his head was sandy-coloured. Dear old Sandy – he grew up into such a faithful, loving dog.'

'Dad, I want a puppy!' said John suddenly,

feeling that he really must have one. It wouldn't be as nice as Dopey, of course – but it would be lovely to have something alive that was his very own to look after and love.

'Well,' began Mr Carlton, who had secretly wanted a dog for ages, 'well, I don't see why . . .'

'Oh, Peter! It's bad enough to begin having cats!' said Mrs Carlton. 'Not dogs too, please. Marian will say she wants a parrot or something next.'

'I shan't,' said Marian. 'If anybody is going to give me a pet, I'll have a baby, please. I do think the Taggertys are lucky to have a baby.'

'Oh, those Taggertys!' groaned Mrs Carlton. 'Why must you want everything the same as they have?'

'Can I have a puppy for my birthday – or better still, for Christmas, because it's nearer?' asked John again, his eyes shining. 'Mum, it won't be any bother, really it won't.'

'It will chew up the rugs, make messes all over the place, bark and yelp and whine, upset things and be a real nuisance in the garden,' said Mrs Carlton.

'Well,' said John, looking suddenly sad, 'if it will upset you, Mum, I won't ask again. I can always share Dopey.'

'Oh, Dopey might as well be our dog as the Taggertys',' said Mrs Carlton, 'the way he comes in at every hour of the day. He even came in yesterday when I was knitting all by myself here, and ran off with my ball of wool. He pulled my knitting right out of my hands.'

The children roared. 'Oh, I wish I'd seen him,' said Annette. 'Oh, Mummy, John won't ask you again for a puppy, but I shall go on and on asking for him, because I know how much he wants one. And it isn't fair for me to have a kitten if he can't have a puppy.'

Mrs Carlton looked round at the four earnest faces. Mr Carlton was gazing at her, too. She suddenly put down her knitting and began to laugh.

'Don't look at me like that!' she said. 'You look like a lot of Dopeys, all gazing at me with big, doggy eyes. Don't! You shall have your puppy if you want him so much, John. I know Daddy will be thrilled to have a dog to go with him for walks, too.'

There was an outburst of delighted squeals and shouts, and three children flung themselves on Mrs Carlton with all their might. She was squeezed and hugged till she had no breath left.

'And now I'll have my turn,' said Mr Carlton, and gave her a hug, too. 'Thank you for giving in to us, Alice. I promise you that if the dog is a nuisance we won't keep him.'

'But I bet before long, Mum gets fond of

him,' said John in a low voice to Marian. 'She's already fond of the kitten.'

'So am I,' said Marian. 'I never wanted a dog before, but somehow Dopey has made me change my mind. I think if you really get to know a dog you can't help wanting one yourself. And I do know Dopey now, and though he's quite mad and awfully silly sometimes, I just can't help loving him.'

'You're changing, Marian,' said John, in surprise. 'You used to be so scared of animals. Now you don't seem to mind nearly so much. I hope I get my puppy in time for Christmas, don't you? What a wonderful Christmas it would be!'

'Mummy's changing, too,' said Marian, answering the first part of John's speech. 'Dear me – we've changed the Taggertys quite a lot – and perhaps they've changed us as well!'

16

All Sorts of Things Happen

A lot of things happened the next week. John was top of his form, and his mother was delighted. Pat was bottom, and was forbidden to play in a football match he was really looking forward to, much to his anger.

Whitefeet wandered away and got lost for a whole day and Annette nearly went mad with despair. Maureen found her wandering round the Taggertys' garden, calling miserably, tears streaming down her cheeks.

'Where can Whitefeet be?' asked Maureen, putting her arm round Annette. 'Don't cry so. He'll come back.'

'Pat says he may be stolen,' wept Annette. 'Or he might have got run over. Or . . .'

'Oh, don't listen to what Pat says,' said Maureen impatiently. 'Whitefeet can't be far away.'

'I simply don't know what to do,' said Annette, tears pouring down her cheeks again. 'I've done everything I can.'

'Have you prayed about it?' asked Maureen suddenly. 'God is sure to know where Whitefeet is, isn't He?'

'I never thought of that!' said Annette, and she stood under the weeping willow tree and spoke directly to God whom, she felt sure, was always ready to listen to her, no matter what she said. Maureen stood nearby, listening.

'Dear God, You know where my little kitten is, the one with the white feet like Socks,' said Annette, wiping her tears away. 'Please let me find him. Amen.'

The girls searched everywhere again and Biddy came to join in too. Then Dopey came prancing round. Suddenly he pricked up his ears, and leaped right over the wall into Annette's garden. He began to bark loudly.

'What's the matter with Dopey?' said Maureen. 'He's awfully excited.'

They climbed over the wall to see. Dopey was at the foot of a beech tree, standing with his forefeet up the trunk of the tree. He barked loudly again.

And there came a tiny answering mew. Annette gave a shriek. 'It's Whitefeet! He's up the tree and he can't get down. Oh, Dopey, you are clever. Whitefeet, I'm coming. Stay there till I come.'

Up the tree went Annette, scratching her bare legs against the trunk, her hair catching in the twigs, and a branch tearing at her shorts. But Annette didn't notice any of these things at all.

Up she went till she came to where the terrified
little kitten sat, clinging to a swaying branch.

'Whitefeet! How long have you been up here?
Fancy climbing up when you can't climb down!'
cried Annette, taking the kitten gently by the
fur at the back of its neck. She placed it on her
shoulder, where it at once dug in its claws. But
Annette didn't mind. Whitefeet could scratch
her to pieces for all she cared.

Down she went, and soon they were petting the kitten, and Dopey was trying to nose his way in too and share in the excitement, his long tail lashing against the girls' bare legs.

Annette rubbed her eyes. Her face was stained and smeary, her hair was dirty and torn. She might have been a Taggerty! But she was very happy because she had found her precious kitten, and had climbed a tree to rescue him. 'I thought he was gone for ever,' she said, cuddling him.

Maureen was very thoughtful after this little happening. God heard Annette's prayer, she thought. It was almost like a miracle. I think I'll go to Sunday School with Marian, and I think I'll say some prayers too.

So, much to Marian's surprise, and to Pat's real amazement, Maureen went off to Sunday School with Marian and John and Annette on the next Sunday. She liked it. She liked the teacher, who told them the story of the boy with the loaves and fishes, and she wished she had been that boy, who had some little fish and bread to take to Jesus to feed all the hungry people.

'I'm going to say my prayers now, too,' she told Marian. 'Can I just say them in bed, or is it best to kneel down? Does it matter?'

'Well, it's best to kneel down properly,' said

Marian. 'It seems more reverent somehow, and you can think what you're doing then, too. It's so easy to fall asleep in bed.'

It was rather difficult for Maureen to say her prayers at night, because as soon as Pat discovered she was doing so he teased her. 'Little goody-goody! Look, Dopey, lick Maureen's feet! They're nice and bare, turned up all ready for you.'

Then Dopey's tongue would lick Maureen's upturned feet, and she would wriggle and squeal, because she was very ticklish there. 'You're mean, Pat! God will be angry with you. Take Dopey away.'

A little ashamed of himself, Pat did take Dopey away. Maureen prayed very fervently, and Biddy was curious to know what she was praying for. But Maureen wouldn't tell her. She wasn't going to be laughed at by Pat or Biddy.

During the next week Marian noticed that Maureen was very quiet. 'Is anything wrong?' she said. 'Don't you feel well? You don't think you're going to be ill, do you?'

'No,' said Maureen. 'It's only that I keep on and on asking God for things and He never listens to me at all. It's not much use saying prayers, really.'

'What did you ask Him for?' asked Marian.

'Well, you know that test paper we had last

week?' said Maureen. 'One of the questions was "Where is the river Amazon?" and I put down that it was in Italy, but it's in South America. So I prayed to God to make it be in Italy because that was the only question I got wrong.'

Marian stared at Maureen in surprise. 'But Maureen! What a thing to ask! Just imagine what would have happened if your prayer had been granted. Think of the river Amazon flowing through Italy all of a sudden. You're silly.'

'You said the other day that nothing was impossible to God,' Maureen said half sulkily. 'Well, He could do that then, couldn't he?'

'He wouldn't want to,' said Marian. 'Be sensible, Maureen. Would a great loving Father like God do a stupid miracle asked for by a girl who had made a mistake in a test paper? Your idea of God is all wrong.'

'I shan't pray any more,' said Maureen, crossly. 'It's difficult enough, anyhow, with Pat teasing me, and Dopey waiting to lick the soles of my feet, and Biddy keeping on asking me what I'm praying for, and you saying that God won't listen to me, and . . .'

'He will, He will,' said Marian. 'But you don't know what to pray for, nor how to pray either, I should think. You don't understand, Maureen. You see, our mother told us lots of things when we were little, and she taught us our prayers, and everything – but nobody has taught you, have they? But you can learn, if you want to. You come to church with us.'

But Maureen wouldn't do that, though she went to Sunday School, and soon Biddy came too. Biddy loved it. Pat wouldn't hear of going.

'I'm happy as I am,' he said to Maureen. 'You shut up. You're not going to make me into a little goody-goody.'

'John isn't like that,' said Maureen.

'He used to be,' said Pat, 'till he got to know us. We've done him a lot of good. I heard his father tell Dad that last week, so there!'

'Uncle Peter is nice,' said Maureen. 'I like him. I wish I could go off on a long walk with him too, on Saturday afternoons, like you and John and Dopey do.'

'Well, you can't,' said Pat. 'Girls not wanted! Especially little goody-goodies!'

The term went on. Pat's work was still bad, and once more he was forbidden to play in an important match as a punishment for slack work.

'It's no good, Taggerty,' said his master, tapping the blue-pencilled page before him. 'I won't have work like this. This isn't homework. Why, even a kindergarten child could do better than this. I shall send in a report to your father soon, if you don't do better.'

Pat scowled. He was ashamed of being

bottom of the form, and out of the match, though he wouldn't try to do better. He vented his annoyance on Maureen, Biddy and Michael, and teased them continually. Michael howled. Biddy was almost in tears. Maureen ran off to the Carltons.

'What is wrong with Patrick lately?' wondered Mrs Taggerty. 'So rude and selfish and noisy! What can be the matter with him?'

They soon knew for a letter came from the headmaster, telling Mr Taggerty of Pat's bad work at school, and asking his father to take him away the next term, or to insist that Pat did better.

It was a great shock to both his parents. They had been proud of their good-looking Patrick, proud of his fearlessness and his prowess at

games. Now, apparently, he was nobody to be proud of at all for in that same letter the headmaster had complained of Pat's untruthfulness and his deceitfulness too! 'He will cheat if he can, and he will tell untruths to get himself out of trouble,' said the letter. 'He is not a desirable influence to have in the school.'

Poor Mrs Taggerty was so shocked and amazed that she sank down into a chair looking white and troubled. 'Our Pat!' she said. 'It can't be!'

'It's partly our fault,' said Mr Taggerty. 'We let them do too much as they liked. We've been so afraid of fussing them too much that we've gone too far the other way – we haven't guided Pat enough, and he's so young he's gone the wrong way without knowing it. This is terrible.'

He spoke to Pat about it. The boy was sullen, and because he was ashamed he pretended to be defiant and not to care. Mr Taggerty hardly knew what to do with him.

He thought of Maureen and compared her with Marian. Marian was sweet to Mrs Taggerty, and always at hand to help with the baby. Even Bridget was always singing her praises and saying how helpful she was. But Maureen would never do a thing to help either Bridget or her mother. And there was Biddy too – lovely, curly-haired Biddy, with her dimples and her smiles, a real little tomboy, but never wanting to do anything for anyone but herself. Really, those children seemed to love Dopey better than they loved anyone! Mr Taggerty suddenly felt discouraged and disappointed.

I'll have a talk with Peter, he thought. Those Carlton children may be too much fussed-over, and too prim and proper sometimes, but they certainly are unselfish, kindly children. How do the Carltons do it? What is there in their home that there isn't in ours? There must be something.

'I'm going to bed, dear,' said Mrs Taggerty to him, in a faint voice. 'All this upset has made me feel ill. Bridget will manage Baby. Oh dear – I keep on and on thinking of that dreadful letter, and Patrick's defiant face, and fearing that Maureen and Biddy will turn out the same. I must have been a bad mother.'

'I'll come up and see to you,' said Mr Taggerty. 'Don't worry too much. Tomorrow I'll go and see Peter, and show him this letter. I've no doubt we can do something between us to make things better.'

He went upstairs with poor Mrs Taggerty, who did indeed look ill. When she was in bed, he kissed her. 'Now don't you worry,' he said. 'Things will be better tomorrow.'

But they weren't any better. They grew worse.

17

When Lunch was Late

Pat did not tell John anything about the letter. He went off to school earlier than usual, and John wondered why, because as a rule they always went together. When he saw Pat's sullen face he was surprised. It was not really like Pat to be sullen.

'What's up?' he asked. 'Anything wrong?'

'Nothing,' said Pat, attempting to grin. But it was a very poor sort of grin. There was plenty wrong. Not only that dreadful letter. He had been rude to his father that morning, and had been unkind to his mother at breakfast. She had come down looking pale and tired, and had asked him to call in at the village shop on the way to school with the grocery list, to save her going out that morning.

'I don't pass the shop,' Pat had said rudely.

'I know,' said his mother, 'but it's only a minute out of your way. I'm tired today, and I thought you could easily do that, Pat.'

'Why don't you make Maureen go?' said Pat. 'You're always asking me to do errands. Why shouldn't Maureen?'

'But I do,' Maureen said. 'I do lots more than you.'

'You don't,' said Pat. 'You're lazy. Everyone knows that.'

'I'm not!' said Maureen indignantly. 'I think that's mean of you. I'm not bottom of the form like you, anyway! Dunce!'

Pat gave her a kick under the table, but caught his mother's ankle instead. She gave a cry.

'Sorry,' said Pat, going red. 'I meant it for Maureen.'

Mrs Taggerty was silent and upset. She had hardly slept at all. She looked at Pat sadly, but he would not meet her eyes.

'Well, Maureen, will you call at the shop for me?' she said, not wanting to argue with the defiant Pat.

'I promised Marian I would call for her this morning,' began Maureen, 'I'll go on my way back from school.'

'That will be too late,' said Mrs Taggerty.

'Biddy can go, surely? She's quite old enough,' said Maureen.

'I don't want to go,' said Biddy, 'I'm going to play shops in the summerhouse.'

'You said you would tidy up your bedroom for me today,' said Mrs Taggerty. 'You've got your dolls' teaset all over the floor.'

'I want to play shops,' said Biddy. 'I don't

want to tidy up the bedroom. Let Maureen do it.'

It was a good thing that Mr Taggerty was not at breakfast, but had gone off some time before to London, or he would certainly have had something to say about all this. Michael began to cry just then, and Mrs Taggerty listened to see if Bridget was going to him. But Bridget was out in the garden hanging up some clothes she had washed, and did not hear him.

'You go, Maureen,' said Mrs Taggerty. 'I expect he just dropped his rabbit out of his cot or something.'

'I shall be late if I bother with Michael,' Maureen said, primly, and ran to get her satchel. Michael went on howling.

Pat went off to school, still sullen. He did not go near the village shop. He wasn't going to run errands for anyone if he didn't want to. Let Maureen go or that lazy little Biddy.

Maureen climbed over the wall to go and call for Marian. She didn't go near the shop either. Biddy never thought of it again. She ran out of the room and into the garden, down to the summerhouse, to play shops with Dopey and with Annette when she came.

Her mother called her after a while, but Biddy pretended not to hear. This was a favourite trick of the Taggertys when they knew they

would be asked to do some job. Presently she heard somebody's footsteps. Biddy ran to a thick bush, crawled under it and sat there perfectly still.

When her mother arrived there was no one to be seen but Dopey, who was sitting on the sunny step of the summerhouse, snapping at a fly that was trying to settle on his nose.

I suppose Biddy has gone over to play with Annette, thought Mrs Taggerty. Naughty little girl, when I wanted her to clear up her bedroom. Now I shall have to stoop down and pick up all those tea-things, just when my head feels like bursting.

She went away, and Biddy crept out of her hiding-place. Dopey greeted her with a lick.

Dopey was very good when the children hid from grown-ups. He never gave them away, but simply sat still where he was, looking very innocent.

Mrs Taggerty saw to Michael, and bathed him, and put him out into his pram after he had been fed. Then she did some of the housework, and at last went to get ready to go out to the village shop.

'You look very pale, Mrs Taggerty,' said Bridget. 'Are you all right?'

'I don't feel too well,' said Mrs Taggerty. 'It must be the heat. It's very hot today, isn't it? I'll leave Michael behind in the garden, Bridget. He'll be all right there.'

She set off with her basket. Biddy saw her go out of the front gate, for she was peeping from behind the side gate, hoping the ice-cream man would come by. He didn't come, and Biddy went down to the bottom of the garden again, where she was playing with Annette, Dopey and Whitefeet. The kitten went everywhere with Annette, and was growing into a playful little thing. He wasn't a bit afraid of Dopey, but smacked him on the nose whenever he sniffed at him, just as Socks did.

The little girls played happily with Dopey and Whitefeet in the summerhouse. They had an array of things to be bought and sold, and first one was the shopkeeper and then the other. Although Annette had been spoilt, and Biddy was a fierce little creature, they played quite well together. If Annette behaved in a spoilt manner, Biddy would fly at her, yelling something rude, so Annette never did behave in a silly way if she played alone with Biddy. And if Biddy lost her temper and became unbearable, Annette would simply climb over the wall and go home, taking Whitefeet with her. So Biddy behaved herself too, because she didn't want to play alone.

A bell rang in the distance. 'Our lunch-bell,' said Annette, getting up, 'I must go. Come on, Whitefeet.'

'Oh, just finish what we're doing,' said Biddy, impatiently, 'you don't need to go at once.'

'Goodbye,' said Annette, 'I'm going.' And she went, carefully putting Whitefeet on the top of the wall while she herself climbed over, and then lifting the kitten down the other side.

John and Maureen arrived home just as Annette went into the house. 'Where's Mum?' said John. 'Oh, there you are, Mum. I got one of my drawings up on the wall today!'

'And I got top marks for needlework,' said Marian. Her mother looked pleased.

'I got top marks for shopping,' said Annette, with a giggle, 'and Whitefeet got top marks for mewing.'

'Idiot!' said John laughing. 'Hello, Whitefeet! Been chasing your own tail this morning?'

Mrs Carlton brought in their lunch, and they sat down hungrily when they came back from washing their dirty hands. 'I bet Pat's hungry for his lunch,' said John to Marian. 'He was kept in at break for not having done his homework, and that means he wasn't allowed to eat the cake he brought.'

Pat was indeed hungry. He ran home from school wondering what there was for lunch. He had already eaten the slice of cake that he was not allowed to eat at break, but that didn't make him feel much less hungry. He joined Maureen, and they went the rest of the way home together. They burst in at the side gate and ran indoors.

Mrs Taggerty wasn't anywhere to be seen. The table was laid for lunch, but there was no sign of Bridget bringing it in, though there was a delicious smell from the kitchen.

Pat ran out to Bridget. 'Why isn't lunch ready? I'm starving! Where's Mum?'

'She's not back yet,' said Bridget, from the stove. 'She went out in a hurry to the village shop, though why to goodness one of you children couldn't have gone for her on the way to school, I don't know!'

'Oh, bother!' said Pat, sniffing the smell that came from the pot on the stove. 'Need we wait for Mum? You can serve us, Bridget – or we can serve ourselves.'

'You can well wait a minute or two for your mother,' said Bridget, sharply. 'And put that spoon down, Patrick. If you go taking bits out of that pot you'll burn the skin off your tongue – though maybe that would be a good thing, the saucy, rude boy that you are!'

'Oh come on, Bridget, dish up lunch,' begged Pat. 'Maureen's starving, too. I don't see why we should wait for Mum. She's probably met some friend and is talking to her, the way she always does.'

'It's mean of her to be late and keep us waiting,' complained Biddy.

'And do you know why she was late going out, Biddy, then?' demanded Bridget, turning round on the little girl. 'She went and tidied up that bedroom of yours, with all those messy little dolls' tea-things on the floor everywhere. It's a thing you should have done yourself. Ah, there's Michael crying. Go and see to him, Maureen.'

'Let him cry,' said Maureen. 'I'm not Marian. I don't want to coo over him at every moment. He's a nuisance.'

'Shame on you to talk that way of your baby brother!' said Bridget sternly, stirring the pot vigorously. 'You don't deserve the kind mother and father you have, nor a blessed darling baby like young Michael there – nor someone like me, either, always slaving for you and never getting a polite word, nor a civil thank you. You're a bad lot, and that's the truth.'

The three Taggertys took no notice. They had heard all this many times before. Usually Bridget then went on to praise the three Carltons and their nice ways. But this time she didn't. She glanced at the clock.

'A quarter past one. Your mother's watch must have stopped, I'm thinking, and she's doing her shopping late, not knowing the time.'

'But the shops shut at one,' said Pat. 'I expect she's gone in to see a friend. You know how Mum talks and talks and talks sometimes.'

'I want my lunch!' wailed Biddy. 'Bridget, can I have a piece of bread? I want my lunch!'

'Go to the front gate, Patrick, and have a look to see if your mother's coming,' said Bridget, looking at the clock again. Pat shot off. He soon came back.

'The road's empty. There's no sign of Mum or anyone else. What can she be doing?'

'You bring in the bread, Maureen, and the jug of water,' said Bridget, making up her mind. 'Go along now. Pat, you get me the hot plates. Biddy, bring in the butter.'

The children did as they were told. Bridget put the lunch on a dish and carried it in herself. The children sat down. Dopey laid himself down under the table, where he could receive unseen all the bits the children didn't like, and where he could lick as many bare legs as he wished.

Bridget served each of the children. Then she glanced at the dining-room clock. It struck half past one as she looked at it. What could be keeping Mrs Taggerty?

The children set to work hungrily to eat their lunch. Bridget put a little on her own plate, but somehow she couldn't eat it. She was worried. Dopey suddenly licked her ankle and made her jump.

Michael yelled again and she went to see him. When she got back the children had finished and were drumming on the table with forks and spoons, impatiently.

'What's for pudding? Say it's sponge pudding! With treacle!' said Pat.

'Well, it's not then. Your mother and I had no time to go making puddings this morning,' said Bridget, gathering up the dirty plates. 'It's stewed plums and custard.'

She brought the dishes in, and served the children again. She looked at the clock. A quarter to two!

'Mummy *is* late!' said Biddy. 'Where can she be?'

'Maybe she's run away from the bad lot of children that you are,' suggested Bridget. Biddy stared at her in alarm.

'No, she wouldn't run away from us! Anyway, she would never leave Michael. Bridget, where *is* she? I want her.'

Bridget was silent. The children looked at her worried face, and fear suddenly made their hearts go cold.

'Something's happened,' said Bridget. 'I feel it in my bones. Yes, something's happened.'

18

A Terrible Shock

The three children sat as if they were turned to stone. Dopey gave a little whine that startled them terribly, for they had all forgotten he was there.

'What do you mean – something's happened?' said Maureen at last, in a whisper.

'She was tired and pale,' said Bridget, 'and she didn't want to go walking out. She looked sad and it was a pity to see her looking like that, for it's not like her. I think I'll go along the road and see if I can meet her.'

'Let me go!' cried Pat, jumping up. But before another word was said the sound of a shrill bell made them all jump.

'The telephone!' said Bridget. 'Now we'll get some news – and pray God it's not what I feel in my bones.' She went to the telephone and picked up the receiver. She put it to her ear. A voice spoke. The children clustered round, listening, 'No, Mr Taggerty is out,' said Bridget. 'He'll not be in till teatime. I'm Bridget, the mother's help. Is there any message I can take for him? Mrs Taggerty is out, too.'

The children listened eagerly and watched Bridget's face. The voice said something else. Bridget gave little gasps of horror and sank down on the chair beside the telephone. Her hand began to tremble.

'Oh, poor Mrs Taggerty! Oh, dear, is she bad? You'd best try and reach Mr Taggerty. He's at his brother's in London. Just a minute.' She looked up the number. 'Yes, the children are here. I'll see to them. You get on to Mr Taggerty, and he'll know what's best to be done.'

She put down the receiver. There were tears running down her cheeks. Maureen clutched at her. 'What's the matter with Mummy? What's happened to her?' Bridget gulped once or twice. All three children were crying, even Pat. Bridget put her arm round Biddy.

'It mayn't be so bad as we think,' she said. 'Your mother was on her way to the village shop, and was just crossing the road there, when she must have come over giddy. I told you she didn't look well. And she fell down in front of a car.'

Biddy screamed. She shook Bridget's arm violently. 'Is she hurt? Is she hurt? You've got to tell us.'

'Yes, she's hurt,' said Bridget, wiping her tears away. 'She's at the hospital. But maybe she's not hurt very badly, so don't let's fret too much till we know.'

'Will she be home tonight?' asked Maureen, who couldn't imagine home without her mother there.

'Oh, no,' said Bridget. 'Of course not. Not for some time. Your poor father! This will be a terrible shock to him.'

Pat was very white. He looked so strange that Bridget drew him into the kitchen and sat him down by the fire in her chair. 'Now don't take on so,' she said. 'There's clever doctors and nurses at that hospital, and she'll soon be home again, right as rain.'

'You don't understand,' said Pat in a whisper. 'She asked me to go to the shop for her – and I wouldn't. It was all because of me she was knocked down.'

Then Maureen flung herself against Bridget. 'I wouldn't go either,' she cried wildly. 'Bridget, I wouldn't go either.'

'Ah, we never know what a moment's selfishness will bring,' said Bridget, wiping her eyes again. 'You've not been kind to your mother lately, and that's the truth.'

Neither Maureen nor Pat would go to school that afternoon, and Bridget hadn't the heart to make them. She telephoned Mrs Carlton who came round at once. Her calm kindness made everyone feel better.

'Now, we mustn't worry till we know there's something to worry about,' she said. 'It's quite certain that Mummy will be in hospital for a little while, at any rate, so we can plan all sorts of things to help her. She mustn't be allowed to worry one moment about anything, because if she does she will take longer to get better.'

Michael began crying again. Everyone had forgotten him in the upset. 'Poor lamb! He'll be wanting his meal,' said Bridget. 'What I'm to do with him I don't know. He'll be crying for his mother all the time. Maureen's no good with him.'

'I will be, I will be!' cried Maureen at once. 'I'll be as good as Marian is. I'll help him, Bridget. I will really.'

'Marian will come and help with him, too, because he loves her,' said Mrs Carlton. 'And I'll come in the mornings. We'll manage, you'll see, till Mrs Taggerty comes back.'

Mrs Carlton took all the children back to tea with her; Michael too. The Carltons were horrified to hear the bad news. They all liked kind, easy-going Mrs Taggerty. Marian took Michael from her mother.

'Oh, Mummy! He'll miss his own mother so much. Mummy, can't we have him here? I could look after him. I know exactly how to. I could even give him his bath, I'm sure.'

'No, I'm going to look after him,' said Maureen. 'Mummy will like to know I'm doing that. He'll be happier at home with us, too.'

Mr Taggerty arrived at his house after tea, after having first gone to the hospital. He was glad to find that the children were not there for the moment. Bridget came to him, her face full of questions and anxiety.

'It's pretty bad, Bridget,' said Mr Taggerty. 'The car hit her when she fell. The shock has been dreadful for her.'

'Will she . . . will she be all right?' asked Bridget, her voice trembling.

'I hope so,' said Mr Taggerty. 'I hope and pray so, Bridget. Where are the children?'

'They're at the Carltons'. That kind Mrs Carlton came and fetched them all,' said Bridget, sniffing and blinking tears away. 'They're terribly upset, of course. Poor Patrick, he went as white as a sheet. He's got some idea that he's to blame for the accident. His mother asked him to go to the village shop for her and he wouldn't. She had to go instead, and it was when she was crossing the road to the shop that the accident happened.'

'Poor Pat. Yes, he will reproach himself terribly for more than one thing,' said Mr Taggerty, thinking of the letter from the headmaster that had upset his wife so much. 'Can you manage, Bridget? Mrs Taggerty won't be back for some time I'm afraid. I could send Pat to my brother's if you could manage the others. We'll get someone to help you.'

'Now, don't you worry your head about anything but Mrs Taggerty,' said kind, loyal Bridget. 'I can manage all right. I can manage fine, and I'll see to the children just as well as their mother did, though maybe I'll be a bit stricter than she is. As for Pat, send him off if you like. He might feel happier away from here.'

But when Mr Taggerty suggested to Pat that he should go away to stay for a while, Pat shook his head at once. 'No, Dad. Don't make me go. I want to stay here, near Mum, so that I can see her when she's getting better. I can help Bridget with the others too. And Dad, I'm – I'm most awfully sorry about that letter, I'll try and do better. Oh, if only Mum comes back quickly I'll be top of the form. I'll do anything, anything! It's all my fault it happened. How could I be so mean to her? It was such a little thing she wanted me to do.'

'Pat, so often the little things grow into great big things,' his father said gravely. 'Well, I shall not send you to Uncle Henry's, if you really will help with the others, and do what you can for Bridget too.'

'Oh, Dad!' said Pat, and flung his arm round his father's neck. 'Dad, I'll help you. Trust me

again, and let me help. And if you see Mum tonight, tell her I'm sorry about everything, and I'll show her I am when she comes back home.'

The next day was a very miserable one for the Taggertys, and for the Carltons too, for they shared wholeheartedly in their friends' sorrow. The news was not good from the hospital, and Mr Taggerty spent the whole day there. The children went to school as usual and everyone was especially kind to the two Taggertys. Pat worked grimly, meaning to make up now for every slack hour he had spent before.

That evening, when the children heard that their mother was not any better, they felt afraid. 'We'd better pray very hard,' said Maureen. 'All of us, not only me. You must too, Pat. It's a pity you've always laughed at me so for praying. But it's the only thing left for us to do now.'

Pat stared at Maureen. 'I don't believe God would bother to listen to me,' he said at last. 'Why should He? I've been beastly. It doesn't seem fair that I should have laughed at the idea of praying, and now, just when we're in trouble, suddenly I think I'd better do it. If I were God I wouldn't listen to people who did that.'

'Yes,' said Maureen. 'It does seem rather small and mean only to pray when you want something very badly, like we do now. I shouldn't think our prayers would be worth much.'

'Yours might,' said Pat. 'But Biddy's and mine wouldn't. Do you think – do you think we could go and ask the Carltons to do some praying, because after all they always do pray anyway, and their prayers would be heard more than ours. It might be of some help if they prayed hard for Mum.'

'Yes, let's go,' said Maureen. 'Let's go now and ask them. I know they won't mind.'

So the three of them climbed over the wall just before Annette's bedtime, with Dopey, and went to find the Carltons.

'Hello!' said John. 'We were just going to come and ask you if you'd like to have supper with us.'

'We've come to ask you something too,' said Maureen, seeing that Pat was tongue-tied. 'John, will you pray for our mother, please? To make her better, you know. Pat and I don't think our prayers would be much good. I'm sure Pat's wouldn't because he's always laughed at the idea. But it's very, very important. We have to do every single thing we can for Mummy.'

The three Carltons looked at the three serious Taggertys. 'But we *are* praying for your mother!' said John. 'How could you think we weren't? We all did last night, and this morning too. Even Annette prayed for a long time. That's the first thing we thought of.'

'Oh,' said Maureen. 'Thank you, John. It's such a relief to know that.'

'But you must pray too,' said John. 'And don't think your prayers won't be heard. They will. Mum says every single prayer is heard, the sinner's and the saint's.'

The three Taggertys looked very much relieved. They couldn't help feeling much better now that they knew the Carltons were doing so much.

'I must get back to Michael,' said Maureen. 'It's his bedtime. You come and help too, Biddy.'

They went off. Pat stayed behind. Annette went in to bed, and Marian decided to climb over the wall and help Maureen with the baby.

Pat was left with John. He looked so woebegone that John wanted to comfort him. 'Cheer up,' he said. 'Maybe the news will be better tomorrow.'

'John,' said Pat, 'I want to tell you something. It's very important. I've been thinking about it all day long. I simply must tell someone!'

19

Pat makes a Solemn Promise

'What is it?' asked John, curious to know why Pat was suddenly so very earnest and solemn. Then it all came out – all about the letter from the head, and how upset his father and mother had been; how he hadn't said he was sorry or anything, how rude and unkind he had been to his mother the morning of the day she had had her accident, and how he had refused to go to the village shop.

'So, you see, I can't help feeling it's all my fault,' said Pat. 'And John – if she doesn't get better, I shall never, never be happy again. Do you think that if I tell God I will turn over a new leaf, and work hard at school, and be good to Mum always and always, and to the others too, He would let her get all right again?'

'I don't know,' said John, slowly. 'I don't see how anyone can make a bargain with God like that. It seems awful cheek, somehow. Like saying, "You do this and I'll do that. And if you won't, I won't." There's something wrong about it somewhere.'

Pat gazed at him in despair. 'Well, there must

be something I can do,' he said. 'And that's the best thing I can think of.'

'Let's go and ask my father about it,' said John, hearing his father in the hall. 'Look, he's gone to sit in the study. Come on, let's ask him.'

They went in. Mr Carlton was surprised to see the solemn faces of the two boys. 'Come to ask me something?' he said. 'Sit down then.'

They sat down, Pat looking worried and nervous. John poured out everything to his father, who listened gravely without saying a word.

'You see, Dad, Pat can't think of anything better, but it does seem a bit as if he's trying to make a bargain with God,' finished John. 'And somehow that seems wrong.'

'You can't bargain with God,' said Mr Carlton. 'And no one should try. What you can do,

Pat, is to do all you say you will, help your family all you can, and be kind and unselfish – whatever may happen to your mother. That isn't a bargain then, you see. It's saying you are really sorry, and that you are going to show it. It's a promise, not a bargain. You would keep that promise even if your mother didn't come back again.'

'I see,' said Pat, his face very serious. 'Yes, I do see that. If I really am sorry, I should be willing to do that, no matter what happens. Well, I will do it. I'll promise. Shall I make my promise to you?'

'No. To God,' said Mr Carlton. 'It's a very solemn thing to do, Pat. Think well about it, before you make it. And ask God for His help in keeping the promise, too. You will not be strong enough to keep it alone.'

The boys went out of the room. Pat gave John's arm a sudden squeeze. 'Isn't your father great?' he said. 'You know, he's an absolute sport – and yet you can go and talk to him about things like this too. Oh, John – I feel a bit happier now I can really *do* something. I shall make my promise tonight before I go to bed.'

Pat kept his word. He made his solemn promise that night and got into bed afterwards feeling happier. He thought about his mother. How could he have been so mean to her? How could he have said he wasn't going to the village

191

shop? Such a small thing to do for anyone you loved! And there were other things too.

There was the time she had asked him to help her untangle her wool when she wanted to wind it into balls, and he had pretended he had forgotten, and had gone out without doing it. There was another time when she had asked him to bring the pram in from the rain, and he hadn't, and it had got soaked. She had asked him for so many little kindnesses, and so many times he hadn't done them.

Not because I didn't love you, Mum, he said to her in his heart. Don't think that, will you? It was only because I didn't think enough. I was unkind and selfish. You were always doing things for me, and I hardly ever did anything for you. But you come back and see what I'll do!

Maureen said long prayers that night. She, too, had felt very remorseful about her unkindness to her mother. She had taken advantage of Mrs Taggerty's easy-going ways. She had told her lies and deceived her. Now Maureen went red in the dark, as she remembered the mean little things she had done.

Why didn't I take Michael out for her the other day? Why did I forget to leave the parcel she asked me to leave? Why didn't I make my bed when she was busy?

Biddy heard her tossing about and muttering.

'What's the matter?' she asked. 'Are you thinking about Mummy? So am I, too.'

'I'm thinking how beastly I was,' said Maureen. 'And you were too, Biddy. We all were, except Daddy – and Michael, but he's too little to be kind or unkind. You didn't clear up those dolls' tea-things for Mummy, did you?'

'No,' said Biddy, in a small voice. 'I didn't. And when Mummy came down the garden and called me, I hid under the bushes and didn't answer. And perhaps I could have gone out for her, instead of her going.'

'We were all horrid,' said Maureen. 'It seems like a terrible punishment for us, doesn't it? Sometimes we've jeered at John and Marian and Annette because they never deceive their mother, or tell her lies, or refuse to do the things she asked them to – but they're right, you know. If you love people, you've got to be decent to them. I wish I'd been decent.'

'So do I,' Biddy said, and began to cry. 'I want Mummy. I want her to come up the stairs this very minute and tell us not to talk, and kiss us goodnight. I don't like all the things that are happening. I feel sort of strange and odd.'

'I do, too,' said Maureen.

They said no more, and after a while Biddy fell asleep. But Maureen kept awake a long time, and Pat even longer. Bridget came in to look at them at ten o'clock, and Pat was still awake.

'You go to sleep now, boy,' said Bridget, kindly. 'We can only hope and pray for the best.'

'Are you praying too, then?' asked Pat.

'Well, of course!' said Bridget. 'I'm a Christian woman, and you should know it, Patrick Taggerty. Now, you go to sleep, and the morning will maybe bring good news.'

The telephone rang next day at breakfast time. Mr Taggerty went to answer it, an anxious look on his face. He said, 'Yes, yes,' several times into the telephone, while the children listened breathlessly. Bridget appeared from the kitchen, her face anxious. Mr Taggerty put the receiver down. He turned to the children, and there was a faint smile on his face. 'Just a bit better news,' he said. 'Mummy's had a fair night – and she has been asking about us. I'll go and see her this morning.'

The children felt as if a load had rolled away from their hearts. If their mother was actually asking about them, she couldn't be so very, very ill. Surely very, very ill people didn't ask about anybody at all?

'Dad, will you buy Mum some flowers for me?' asked Pat, taking down his money-box. 'And some from Maureen and Biddy too – and a tiny bunch from Michael? And give her our very best love, and tell her we are all thinking of her and – and – loving her very much.'

'I will,' said Mr Taggerty, and Pat saw the shine of tears in his father's eyes.

Poor Daddy, he thought. This is awful for him. I'll never let him down again. It's not fair.

Dopey seemed to feel the better news too, and became more his old self. He had been very subdued and had gone about with his big tail down and his ears pressed back, which gave him a very odd look. He couldn't understand where Mrs Taggerty was. He had looked for her everywhere.

'Better news, Dopey,' said Pat, and at the sound of the boy's more cheerful voice, Dopey rolled over on his back and did his bicycling act. Socks sat washing herself near by, watching Dopey scornfully. She thought him a very silly dog, though she didn't mind playing with him sometimes when she felt like it.

Mr Taggerty came back from the hospital looking a little more cheerful. Bridget met him at the door.

'Well, the news is no worse,' said Mr Taggerty. 'She's worried about us all, though, which is such a pity. You must go and see her tomorrow, Bridget, and tell her we're all getting on famously, and she must hurry up and get better.'

'What about the children?' asked Bridget. 'Can they see her too? Once they see her again they won't worry so much.'

'Well – she's got a big bandage round her head,' said Mr Taggerty. 'It would scare them to see that. We'd better wait till it's off and she's feeling a bit better.'

The next day came and the next. Mrs Taggerty began to mend. The children were as good as gold. They did their very best to think of all kinds of ways to help Bridget and their father. Even Biddy tried.

Maureen amazed Bridget by the way she took charge of little Michael. It was true that Marian came to help, and even felt a little jealous when she saw how well Maureen was managing – but certainly Michael was well looked after, and hardly cried at all.

Pat surprised his masters at school by suddenly working harder than anybody. He was keeping his promise, and nothing was going to make him break it. And he wanted to do more still. What could he do?

I'll clear away all the weeds from the part of the garden near the windows, where Mum likes to sit, he thought. I'll weed the path there, too. She'd like that. She's always said how nice it would look if only she could get down to the weeding. Well, I'll do it for her, for a surprise

when she comes back. When she comes back!
Doesn't that sound good?

Biddy wanted to do something too. So she
borrowed a pail of water from Bridget and a
cloth and scrubbing brush and soap, and began
to clean out the little summerhouse with a great
deal of splashing. 'Mummy can sit here when

she comes back,' she told Bridget. 'She always said she wouldn't because it was so dusty and dirty. I'll make it clean for her.'

Mrs Carlton helped a lot by having the children in to meals at times, to give Bridget a rest. Everyone was very kind, even Miss Johnson next door, who had never had a good word to say of the Taggertys since they had moved in.

'People are good when trouble comes along,' said Bridget. 'You never know who your friends are till something happens.'

She glanced at Pat, who was cleaning the pram for her. And you never know what good there is in people till trouble brings it out, she thought. Look at that boy – I never knew anyone change so. But will it last? It all depends on himself.

The news grew better and better. At last the bandages were off and Mr Taggerty said that he would take the three children to see their mother the very next day. They were overjoyed.

'It's ages since we saw her,' said Pat. 'Maureen, I hope to goodness you've got clean clothes to wear.'

'Well, I have,' said Maureen. 'And so has Biddy. And Bridget has washed your blue shirt and pressed your trousers. We'll look as nice as the Carltons tomorrow!'

'I'll see that you do!' said Bridget. 'Your

mother will have told everyone her three children are coming and she'll want to be proud of the lot of you. You'll go with your hands clean, and your faces and knees clean, and your hair brushed, and your nails clean too. Do you hear me, Patrick, my boy? Your nails clean, too!'

Pat laughed. 'All right. I'll see they are. I'm just as anxious to make Mum think we look nice as you are, Bridget. It's the one time we shan't grumble about it!'

And indeed, they did look nice when they set off with their father the next day. 'I'm quite proud of my family,' he said. 'I've never seen you look like this before. I really feel that your name must be Carlton, not Taggerty!'

20

Going to see Mrs Taggerty

It was a week since the accident had happened – a long, long week to the three Taggertys. They were all excited at the thought of seeing their mother again, but they somehow felt a little solemn too.

Mrs Taggerty was in a little private room. The nurse opened the door and said, 'Here are the children, Mrs Taggerty – but mind, only ten minutes – and don't get excited or I'll take them away!'

The children did not dare to do as they would have liked to do – rush in and fling themselves on their mother. They tiptoed in, wide-eyed and quiet. Mrs Taggerty was lying in bed, very pale. The big bandage had gone, and only a small one was left. There was a bruise on her right cheek where she had fallen. The children couldn't bear to see it there. She smiled at them, with tears of joy in her eyes.

'Hello, darlings! Aren't I silly to be like this! But I'll soon be better.'

Biddy put her face down by her mother's on

the pillow and pressed her soft cheek against hers. 'Mummy, I love you! Mummy, are you hurt? When will you come back? I'm sorry I didn't clear up the dolls' tea-things for you.'

Maureen could not say a word except for a choked-out 'Hello, Mummy! Are you better?' She stroked her mother's soft, wavy hair with trembling fingers.

Poor Pat opened his mouth to speak but not one word would come out. He gazed at his mother as if he could not look at her enough, and he knew in that one minute how much she loved him, and how much he loved her. I didn't mean to be horrid to you, his eyes said to her.

I'm terribly sorry I didn't do the errand you wanted me to. It's all my fault. And oh, I kicked you too that morning, though I didn't mean to. Somehow I can't say a word to you, but you *must* understand, you've *got* to understand.

And his mother understood. She squeezed his rough little brown hand very hard and smiled through her tears looking very happy. 'It's all right, Patrick,' she said. 'I know what you're feeling and thinking, darling. We'll be happy together again when I come home. Now tell me about Michael. Is he missing me very much?'

'We all do,' said Maureen. 'Mummy, it's strange without you. You've always been there, and now you're not. I'm looking after Michael for you.'

'Yes, Bridget told me,' said Mrs Taggerty. 'I'm so glad.'

The ten minutes went far too quickly. Biddy was really indignant when the nurse came to shoo them out. 'Why, we haven't had *one* minute!' she said to the nurse. 'And we haven't tired Mummy.'

The nurse glanced at Mrs Taggerty. She was looking happy but very pale. 'You must all go now,' she said briskly. 'Say goodbye. You can come again next week.'

'Goodbye,' said Mrs Taggerty. 'You do all look so very nice and neat. I hope everyone in the hospital is looking out of the window when you go by!'

The children went, and Mr Taggerty slipped into the room to stay for a while with his wife. She could hardly speak, she was so tired, but he saw she was happy.

'They're the nicest – children – in the world,' she whispered, and took her husband's hand in hers.

The Taggertys were so relieved at actually having seen their mother again, having felt her warm hand and heard her soft, familiar voice, that their feelings got the better of them as soon as they left the hospital and found Dopey waiting for them outside the gates, where Mr Taggerty had tied him up.

'Dopey! She's getting better!' Biddy yelled, and ran to untie him. 'Hurrah!'

They tore home at top speed, Dopey leaping and bounding madly. They ran headlong into Mrs Wilson and Miss Johnson as they turned the corner to go to their house. They almost knocked them over. The shopping basket flew out of Miss Johnson's hand and Dopey pounced on it with joy. He took it by the handle very cleverly and pranced down the road. Biddy squealed with laughter.

'Oh, look at Dopey! He's gone shopping!'

Miss Johnson looked at the children in

disgust. 'To think they race along the road like this, shouting and laughing, when their poor mother's lying ill in hospital!' she said to Mrs Wilson.

A week or two before Pat would have yelled as loudly as Biddy, and would have rushed off laughing to think of the collision they had had. But he didn't do that now.

He spoke to Maureen. 'Go and get the basket from Dopey.' Then he turned to the two disapproving ladies. 'I'm so sorry we nearly knocked you over. You see – we've just been to see our mother in hospital, and we felt so glad she was getting better than we just galloped along the road in joy!'

Maureen came up with the basket. She gave it to Miss Johnson. 'I'm sorry we gave you a fright,' she said. 'Thank you for all your kindness about Mummy, Miss Johnson. Daddy said you sent her some lovely flowers.'

Miss Johnson forgot her crossness and smiled. 'I'm glad she's better. I am going to see her myself next week, I hope.'

'Could you tell her we're getting on all right?' said Maureen. 'So that she won't worry about us?'

'I'll tell her you're being extra-specially good!' said Miss Johnson. 'I've seen you wheeling that baby brother of yours out every day, Maureen.

Quite a little mother to him, aren't you?'

The children ran home to tell Bridget about the ten precious minutes at the hospital. Bridget was making cakes and she stirred the mixture and listened with great interest. 'And did you tell her you were all as good as gold?' she asked, stirring vigorously. 'A bad lot, you were, but you're good at heart, and that's worth something. Now stop putting your finger into the bowl, Biddy, do!'

'It tastes so nice,' said Biddy, licking her finger. 'Can I scrape the bowl when you've finished, Bridget? Mummy always lets me.'

'Your mother was too soft with you,' said Bridget. 'There were times when I thought you hadn't one scrap of love for her between you. But maybe there's good in you after all. Will you stop poking your finger into my bowl, Biddy, I'll rap you with my wooden spoon if you do it again.'

'Oh, Bridget, you always sound so sharp and cross but I do like you,' said Biddy, leaning against her, and rubbing Bridget's floury arm with her cheek. 'Daddy says he doesn't know what we'd all do without you.'

'Well, there now,' said Bridget, stirring vigorously again, 'what's come over you to say a nice word to poor old Bridget? It's just that you're wanting to scrape out my bowl!'

'It isn't, it isn't,' said Biddy. 'Is it, Pat? Is it, Maureen? We do like Bridget awfully much, don't we?'

'Of course,' said Pat, gruffly. He put a finger into the cake mixture and got a sharp rap with the wooden spoon.

'Shame on you, being such a baby, licking your fingers like that!' cried Bridget, but her eyes twinkled. 'Get away, the lot of you. Come back when I've finished.'

And when they did come back, the cakes were in the oven, baking nicely, and the bowl was still on the table with quite an extraordinary amount of scrapings left in it. The children looked at it in surprise and began running their fingers

round the bowl, licking them in delight.

'Bridget! I do believe you've left an extra lot on purpose!' called Maureen. 'There's never been so much before. Why does cake mixture taste so much nicer before it's cooked than after? Bridget, you have left us a nice lot.'

'And it's on purpose, you think!' scoffed Bridget. 'Would I be as soft as that, now?'

The days went by. Mrs Taggerty was still in hospital, slowly getting better. But it seemed a very long time. Two weeks went by, and then another. It would soon be the middle of November. Would she never come home?

'*When* will she leave hospital?' asked Maureen. 'I want her back. Can't you get her back, Daddy?'

'She will be out of hospital at the end of November,' said Mr Taggerty, 'and then I am taking her away till she is quite all right again. So she won't be home yet.'

Maureen's face fell. 'But, Daddy! All that time! Oh, Daddy – she will be home for Christmas, won't she?'

'I sincerely hope so,' said Mr Taggerty, smiling. 'Oh yes, I think I can promise you that.'

The children were very disappointed to learn that their mother wouldn't be home for so long. Pat talked to John about it. 'There's one thing,' he said, 'it gives me longer to work hard, John, and get a good report. If only it's really good! I could put it on the table on Christmas morning, and then Mum would know I'd done my best.'

'All our weeding will have been wasted,' said John. 'If she doesn't come home till Christmas she won't be able to go into the garden much, and she won't see how nice we've made the top part.'

John had been helping Pat with the garden, and the two boys had cleared away weeds and cut back bushes, and trimmed the path edges well. Now they were busy each day sweeping away the fallen leaves.

'Never mind, she'll see it from the dining-room window,' said Pat. 'Is your father going for his usual walk this afternoon, John – or doesn't he go in dull, miserable weather like this?'

'Of course he's going,' said John. 'I'm going too. I used to hate walking, but now I like it, especially if you come too. And Dopey, of course.'

Pat had a tremendous admiration for John's father. Neither of them had ever said any more about Pat's solemn promise, but Pat knew that Uncle Peter, as he called Mr Carlton, was watching him week by week, and was glad that he was keeping his word.

All three Taggertys went to Sunday School with the Carltons now. Pat had joined them one Sunday afternoon without a word. The two girls went to church with John, Marian and Annette too, and their parents, and Pat came once or twice.

'I might come always,' he said to John, 'only somehow I can't bear to leave Dopey both morning and afternoon too. I do wish he could go to church as well. I'm sure it would do him good, even if it only taught him to be a bit quieter. I'm trying to make him quiet for when Mum comes home.'

Maureen was managing Michael beautifully, and he crowed to her and held out his arms whenever she came back from school. She was pleased.

'He doesn't seem a nuisance any more,' she said to the half-jealous Marian. 'Isn't it strange?'

'Well, I thought it was strange when you said he was a nuisance!' said Marian. 'Do let me hold him, Maureen. You hardly ever let me have him now.'

'He likes me best now, that's why,' said Maureen, a pleased look on her face.

'He doesn't,' said Marian, fiercely. 'Michael, don't you want to come to Marian?'

Michael turned to her and held out his fat arms. 'There you are!' Marian said triumphantly and bent towards him. The baby put one arm round her neck and then one round Maureen's, and held them tightly with surprising strength so that the heads of the two little girls almost met over him.

'He loves you both exactly the same!' said Biddy, who was looking on. 'I love him too.'

'Yes, but you love Dopey best,' said Maureen. 'No, I'm not calling you, Dopey, you idiot. Get down! Oh look Marian, Michael's trying to pat him. Isn't he the cleverest baby in the whole wide world?'

21

Christmas is Coming!

School days went on and on. Time for work, time for play, breakfast, lunch, tea and supper. Bedtime. The weeks flew by happily, and John, Marian and Annette enjoyed them, though Annette did not go to school yet. Biddy came to play with her, to leave Bridget free in the mornings, with only Michael to see to.

Biddy was a careless and destructive little girl, and she and Annette had many a tussle because of the way she treated Annette's dolls and other toys. But gradually she learned to be careful with them and not to break them. She even learned to put them away!

She learned to be tidier and cleaner too, for Mrs Carlton would not allow her to come and play or to have meals with Annette unless she was at least clean and tidy.

'If you wear a hair-ribbon, then tie it up,' she said firmly. 'Or don't wear one at all. And see that your dress has all its buttons done up, and your shoe buckles, too. No, that isn't being fussy, Biddy. It's part of good manners.'

All the Taggertys began to learn better ways

because they were now so much with the Carltons. Maureen learned to like their tidy, pretty house, and began to compare her own untidy home with it – coats thrown down on the floor, papers about, dead flowers in the vases, everything higgledy-piggledy.

It's just because we always throw our things about, and nobody ever bothers to pick them up, till Bridget gets a fit of tidiness and rushes round tidying, she thought. But as soon as she's done that, we all begin throwing things down again. Well, I'm going to copy Mrs Carlton.

She did, and tried to make Pat and Biddy do the same, and be tidy and neat. But they wouldn't, and Pat became very cross with Maureen.

'You can be as tidy as you like,' he cried, 'but don't try to make Biddy and me the same. And if you're so anxious to get things right, well, run round and pick our things up too. We shan't stop you!' And lo and behold, Maureen even did that too, picking up Pat's things and Biddy's without a murmur, tidying Pat's room, putting his books away, and Biddy's toys. Soon the house was a pleasure to come into, and Mr Taggerty noticed it.

'What a good girl Maureen is,' he said to Bridget. 'I do hope they will go on behaving like this when their mother comes back. It would please her so much.'

The time came for Mrs Taggerty to leave the hospital. She was going away with Mr Taggerty. She had said goodbye to the children the day before, when they had gone to see her.

'Do come back in time for Christmas, Mummy!' they had begged her. 'We can't have Christmas without you.'

Now Mr Taggerty wasn't at home either. There was only Bridget, getting a bit tired and sharp of tongue, but someone familiar, who could be depended on for help at any time. She would scold at the sight of a hole in a sock, but would bind up a hurt knee kindly at the same time. She would be cross with Pat for losing his pen, but would go and try to find it for him before he left for school. They couldn't do without Bridget, that was certain.

All kinds of plans were afoot for Christmas. Bridget was making the puddings, and all the children, the Carltons included, had to stir and wish. The Taggertys, of course, wished fervently that their mother would be home for Christmas. John wished for a puppy, though he felt guiltily that he ought to wish that the Taggertys' mother would be home. Annette and Marian wished it for them, however, so he felt it would be all right.

Everyone was making cards and presents. The Taggertys, with Mrs Carlton's help, were making a big streamer to hang over their front door, with WELCOME HOME, MUMMY on it in big red letters. Maureen and Biddy, who hated sewing, took their share in the work, and didn't grumble once. It was for their mother.

'You never used to do a thing for your mother!' said Annette, sewing at a big letter L. 'Not a thing. We used to think you were awful about that. Now you don't seem to mind anything, not even sewing. I remember one time when you told an awful story to your mother, and . . .'

'Shut up,' said Maureen. 'We don't want to

be reminded of things like that. You wait till your mother has something awful happen to her, and see what you feel about things! It makes you different, somehow.'

'All you Carltons are different too, anyway,' put in Biddy unexpectedly. 'Don't you remember what a dreadful tell-tale Annette was?'

'And a crybaby, too,' said Maureen. 'Awful. And John was such a mother's boy – couldn't even climb a tree! And Marian used to scream if Dopey came too near – and she wanted to go home to her mother when she first came to tea.'

Neither Annette nor Marian liked this kind of remembering. Had they really been like that? Yes, they had. They looked uncomfortable, and Marian went very red.

Maureen saw her scarlet cheeks. 'Don't let's remember horrid things,' she said, giving Marian a little poke. 'You could remember lots about us – how we told the most awful lies and how rough we were, and didn't know our table manners! Don't let's remember them. You showed us how beastly we were, anyway.'

'And you showed us how silly *we* were,' said Marian, generously. 'I never thought we'd be friends.'

'I've finished my letter L,' said Annette. She gave an enormous sigh. 'I must have a rest. Why are needles so small to hold? I'd like a much bigger one. Look at Whitefeet, Maureen. Do look. He's gone to sleep between Dopey's front paws! Oh, I do wish he wouldn't grow so fast. I want him to be a kitten for always.'

John hadn't said any more about a puppy. He was very much hoping for one at Christmas, but he didn't dare to ask about it in case it wasn't to be. But he couldn't help hoping.

The holidays came. Only four more days till Christmas now! The school reports came in. John's was excellent, and so was Marian's. Their parents read them out loud to them, as they always did.

'I wonder what Pat's report is like,' said John. 'I hope it's good. It ought to be because Pat has really tried hard for weeks.'

Mr Taggerty paid a flying visit to his home three days before Christmas, to make arrangements with Bridget about bringing back Mrs Taggerty. She was still an invalid, but otherwise a great deal better.

Pat's report had arrived, and so had Maureen's. Mr Taggerty opened them.

Maureen had quite a good one, and the remark at the bottom pleased her very much:

Has improved tremendously in manners and appearance lately, wrote her form mistress. *Maureen is not nearly so untidy and careless now.*

Pat's report was splendid. His father read it with great pleasure, and then beckoned Pat to him. 'You must read this with me, Patrick,' he said. 'Look at the list of marks you had in the first few weeks, and your position in form – bottom! And now look how the marks go up and up and up and your position in form goes up, too, till you are fourth from the top! And read what your form master has to say of you.'

Pat read the piece at the bottom, his heart beating fast, for his report meant a good deal to him that term.

Patrick seemed quite impossible in every way, except at gym and football, at the beginning of the term, said the report, *and I considered him a very bad influence. Now, I am happy to say, he is quite a different boy, has worked extremely hard and well, is no longer undependable, but trustworthy and honest, a credit to his class, and will, we hope, be a credit to the school as the terms go on. He deserves great praise for being able to change himself in this way, and I am proud of him.*

Pat's face glowed. His father drew him to him. 'I'm proud, too, Pat,' he said. 'Very proud. You have more than made up for the beginning of the term. How pleased your mother will be. We'll put this on her breakfast tray for her on Christmas morning. It will be the best Christmas present she could have!'

Mrs Taggerty was to come home the afternoon before Christmas Day. The children all made great preparations. Bridget cooked and baked hard. All the children's clothes were clean and mended. Baby Michael looked beautiful in a new white woollen suit, knitted by Mrs Carlton.

The big white streamer, with its WELCOME HOME, MUMMY in big red letters, was carefully put up over the front door. There was a special cake with the same words on it in Bridget's best icing writing. There were silver balls, preserved violets, and little yellow sweets all over the icing, too. It looked a lovely cake.

Mr Taggerty's car drew up at the door. Out stepped Mrs Taggerty on her husband's arm, her face radiant. How much better she looked now! The children ran down the path and flung themselves on her.

'Welcome back, Mummy! You've really come!'

'Careful, careful,' said Mr Taggerty. 'Down, Dopey. Bless the dog, he's gone mad. Down, boy, *down*!'

Mrs Taggerty was so glad to be home again that the tears rolled down her cheeks. She looked round as she walked inside. 'How lovely it looks! How tidy and clean everything is! Why, Bridget, there you are! How can I thank you for all you've done! Where's my little Michael?'

It was a lovely homecoming. Everyone enjoyed it, even the three Carlton children, who had gone round by the road and were watching from the pavement on the opposite side. They hadn't wanted to go any nearer for they knew that this was the Taggertys' joyful day, not theirs. But they just wanted a little share of it.

Michael squealed with delight when his mother picked him up. 'Oh, he's grown! He's beautiful!' cried Mrs Taggerty. 'How well he's looking. You have taken great care of him for me, Bridget.'

'Maureen's done her share, Mrs Taggerty,' said Bridget. 'Such good children they've been. You can be proud of them.'

'Why, you always said what a bad lot they were!' said Mrs Taggerty, smiling.

'Well, they are,' said Bridget, twinkling at the three children clustered round their mother. 'A real bad lot – but they're worth their weight in gold, all the same!'

Christmas Eve, with Mummy sitting in her usual chair again – the children could hardly believe it was true. And how nice to have her to come up and kiss them tonight!

Pat had told no one but John and John's father about the solemn promise he had made. But that night, with his arms round his mother, he told her. 'It wasn't a bargain,' he said, hugging her. 'It wasn't something I said I'd do if you came back again, or till you came back again – it was a promise made for always, whatever happened. You'll see I kept my promise, Mum, when you read my report tomorrow morning – and you'll see it when you get my report next term, and the term after, and always! And I'll never, ever be unkind to you again.'

'Oh yes you will – but I shan't mind, and you'll always be sorry and make it up to me again,' said his mother.

Christmas morning was lovely. There were all

kinds of presents on the table, and these were saved up till Mrs Taggerty came down after breakfast to help them to open them. The children had already had stockings, but they were only filled with small things. The real presents were on the Christmas table.

'Oh, what a lovely doll!' squealed Biddy. 'Mummy did you make the clothes?'

'Yes, I had such a long time in bed,' said Mrs Taggerty. 'Oh, who gave me this beautiful mat? Maureen, you don't meant to say you *made* it – and embroidered all these daisies on it too. Well, I am pleased!'

'Dopey's given you something,' said Biddy. 'You haven't opened it yet.'

Mrs Taggerty opened the parcel and everyone yelled with laughter. It was a big bone! 'Oh, Dopey!' she said. 'How can you possible spare it? You must share it with me.'

And Dopey was only too pleased, of course. He didn't understand that it was Christmas. He only knew that everyone was very happy and glad, so he was too. His big tail wagged without stopping.

Then Mrs Taggerty opened Pat's report. Her eyes shone as she read it. 'It's my nicest present,' she said to Pat. 'You couldn't have given me a better one. I like it more than the napkin ring you made me in your craftwork class

– and I do like that very much indeed.'

'I wonder how the Carltons are getting on,' said Pat. 'Mum, we've got a wonderful present for them. At least, he's for John really, but they'll all share him. We're fetching him this morning, in a short while. He's at the farm.'

'It's a spaniel puppy,' said Biddy, unable to keep the secret any longer. 'We bought him between us for the Carltons, but Daddy paid the most money. He's lovely, lovely, lovely.'

They went to fetch the puppy. He was glossy black, with drooping ears and melting brown eyes. In fact, as Maureen said, he was altogether beautiful.

'Not more beautiful than Dopey!' said Biddy

jealously. Dopey was not beautiful, but all the Taggertys thought he was.

'We'll have to hurry,' said Maureen, as they left the farm with the spaniel capering round them, and Dopey making darts at him. 'You know we said we'd go to Christmas Day church with the Carltons this morning. We've got to say a big thank you there for getting Mummy back. Hurry up!'

They hurried. The spaniel hurried too, pleased to run with the children. Pat had tied a label round his neck, giggling as he did so. The spaniel thought it must be his name. But it wasn't.

They went round by road to the Carltons – and, hurrah, there were John, Marian and Annette just starting to go round to *them*.

'We've got a present for you!' yelled Biddy. 'Look! It's this puppy. It's for all of you, but especially for John.'

And John, who had been surprised and disappointed at the non-appearance of a puppy after all for his Christmas present, gave a yell as loud as Biddy's. He dropped down on one knee beside the spaniel, who licked his nose with a little pink tongue.

'Oh! So this is what Biddy and Maureen were so mysterious about! They kept on and on hinting to me and I was too stupid to understand. Isn't he marvellous? I'll call him Scamper, because look how he scampers. Biddy, Pat, Maureen, thank you, thank you, *thank* you!'

Then John looked at the label round the puppy's neck, tied to his scarlet collar. He read it and roared with laughter. 'Look, Annette, look, Marian – see what the Taggertys have written, "Happy Christmas to THOSE DREADFUL CHILDREN"!'

'And look what we've written on our label to you!' squealed Annette, pushing a marvellous conjuring set into Pat's hands. 'Do look!'

Pat looked and laughed. 'You've written just the same!' he cried. '"Happy Christmas to THOSE DREADFUL CHILDREN"!'

'That's what we used to call each other,' said John. 'However could we have? Come on, let's show Mum my puppy. Come on, Scamper, come to your home.'

In at the gate the spaniel scampered, his tail wagging and his ears flapping. Dopey dashed after him, almost knocking him over. All the children followed.

'Happy Christmas, Mrs Carlton!' yelled Biddy, and the others joined in.

And we will wish them a happy Christmas too, and leave them to their lovely Christmas Day. Happy Christmas, dreadful children, happy Christmas to you all!